Praise for Lisa Moore's OPEN

"I got swept up in the sheer snap, crackle and pop of [Lisa Moore's] stories. Her splicing of time and memory. Her fabulous lists. The eroticism of every-day life. She puts all five senses on high alert, 'at alarming speed: falling awake' as she says."

— Shelagh Rogers, *Globe and Mail*

"Lisa Moore's stories are electric with the intensity of the lived and observed moment, and they evoke a passionate response. *Open* leads the list of our top 25 fiction picks for the year."

— Amazon.ca

"Moore's talent is staggering, her images arresting, her dialogue, particularly between men and women, needle-to-the-eye sharp."

— *Maclean's*

"Whether Moore is describing the path of a storm . . . or a girl's first orgasm . . . she has a genius for nailing the physical world on the page. One image after another is a feat of seeing, of waking up the senses. . . . cryptic and passionate."

— Marni Jackson, *Globe and Mail*

"Moore opens scenes as if they were oysters, reveals the meat and juice of life, in all their messy succulence, and finds in the course of her revelation the occasional unexpected — and startlingly beautiful — pearl. . . . The stories are full of nerve and verve. They brim with an irresistible mix of adrenaline, compassion and insight. . . . perceptive and wonderful."

— *National Post*

"These are stories to lose yourself in, and maybe to find yourself in, as well. . . . Every year, there are about a hundred books about exactly the same thing. And every year there is one like this that will knock you flat. . . . Lisa Moore, Lisa Moore, Lisa Moore. Remember that name."

— *Vancouver Sun*

". . . accomplished, polished . . . powerfully visual . . . Moore's riffs hold us rapt by being so arresting."

— *Quill & Quire*

"Observant, witty, genuine and resonant, *Open* is a significant collection on the Newfoundland and national literary stages. This is very good work."

— St. John's *Telegram*

OPEN

STORIES

LISA MOORE

ANANSI

First published in hardcover in 2002 by House of Anansi Press Ltd.

This edition published in 2003 by
House of Anansi Press Inc.
110 Spadina Ave., Suite 801
Toronto, ON, M5V 2K4
Tel. 416-363-4343
Fax 416-363-1017
www.anansi.ca

Distributed in Canada by
Publishers Group Canada
250A Carlton Street
Toronto, ON, M5A 2L1
Tel. 416-934-9900
Toll free order numbers:
Tel. 800-663-5714
Fax 800-565-3770

07 06 05 04 03   1 2 3 4 5

NATIONAL LIBRARY OF CANADA CATALOGUING IN PUBLICATION DATA

Moore, Lisa Lynne, 1964–
Open : stories / Lisa Moore.

ISBN 0-88784-179-1 (bound).—ISBN 0-88784-684-x (pbk.)

I. Title.

PS8576.O61444O64 2002   C813'.54   C2002-900331-8
PR9199.3.M647O64 2002

Cover design: Bill Douglas @ The Bang
Typesetting: Brian Panhuyzen
Printed and bound in Canada

Canada Council   Conseil des Arts
for the Arts   du Canada

*We acknowledge for their financial support of our publishing program the Canada Council for the
Arts, the Ontario Arts Council, and the Government of Canada through the Book Publishing
Industry Development Program (BPIDP).*

Contents

Melody   *1*

Mouths, Open   *25*

The Way the Light Is   *37*

Craving   *59*

Natural Parents   *69*

Close Your Eyes   *97*

Azalea   *107*

If You're There   *121*

The Stylist   *137*

Grace   *153*

Acknowledgements   *217*

Melody

- I -

Melody lets the first half dozen cars go by; she says she has a bad feeling about them.

The trip will take as long as it takes, she says. There are no more cars for an hour. She pulls her cigarettes out of her jean jacket and some matches from the El Dorado. We had been dancing there last night until the owner snapped on the lights. The band immediately aged; they could have been our parents. They wore acid-washed jeans and T-shirts that said ARMS ARE FOR HUGGING, VIVA LA SANDINISTA, and FEMINIST? YOU BET!!!

Outside the El Dorado two mangy Camaros, souped up for the weekend Smash Up Derby, revved their engines and tore out of the parking lot. I watched their tail lights swerve and bounce in the dark. They dragged near the mall and sparks lit the snagged fenders. A soprano yelp of rubber and then near silence. I could smell the ocean far beyond the army barracks. The revolving Kentucky Fried Chicken bucket still glowing in the pre-dawn light. Waves shushing the pebble beach; Brian Fiander falling in beside me. He had been downing B52s. He was lanky and discombobulated until his big hand clasped my shoulder and his too long limbs snapped into place like the poles of a pup tent.

⌒

The clock radio in my dorm room came on in the early afternoon and I listened to the announcer slogging through the temperatures across the island. Twenty-nine degrees. Mortification and the peppery sting of a fresh crush. I'd let Brian Fiander hold my wrists over my head against the brick wall of the dorm while he kissed me; his hips thrusting with a lost, intent zeal, the dawn sky as pale and grainy as sugar. Brian Fiander knew what he was doing. The recognition of his expertise made my body ting and smoulder. My waking thought: I have been celebrated.

I felt logy and grateful. Also sophisticated. I'd had an orgasm, though I didn't know it at the time. I didn't know *that's* what that was. I could count on one hand the number of times I'd said the word out loud, though I'd read about it. I believed myself to be knowledgeable on the subject. I'd closed my eyes while Brian touched me and what I'd felt was like falling asleep, except in the opposite direction and at alarming speed: falling awake. Wildly alert. Falling into myself.

2

I made my way down the corridor to the showers, the stink of warming Spaghetti-Os wafting from the kitchenette. Wavy Fagan passed me in her cotton candy slippers and she smirked. I had a crowbar grin; his hand on my breast, slow, sly circles. Wavy smirked and I knew: *Oh that's what that was.*

The showers were full of fruity mist. Brenda Parsons brushing her teeth. Her glasses steamed. She turned toward me blindly, mouth foaming toothpaste. She had been going out with Brian Fiander.

We can see anything that's coming long before it arrives, and nothing's coming. The highway rolls in the sulky haze of mid-afternoon and Melody and I are eternally stuck to the side of it. The night before comes back in flickers. A glass smashing, swimming spotlights, red, blue. Hands, buttons. The truck, when it appears, is a lisping streak, there and not there as it dips into the valleys. A black truck parting the quivering heat. A star of sunlight reaming the windshield.

I say, Do I stick my thumb out or what?

I'll do the thinking, says Melody. She ties the jean jacket around her waist in a vicious knot. We don't hitch but the truck pulls over. I run down the highway and open the door. Melody stays where she is, she just stands, smoking.

My friend is coming, I say. I climb up onto the bouncy seat. The guy is a hunk. A happy face on his sweatshirt. Smokey sunglasses. Brian Fiander barely crosses my mind. Brian is too willing and skinny; he's unworthy of me.

3

This guy tilts the rearview mirror and puts his hand over the stick shift, which vibrates like the pointer of a Ouija board. He has a wedding ring but he can't be more than twenty. A plain gold band. The fine hair on his fingers is blonde and curls over the ring, catching the light, and I almost lean toward him so he will touch my cheek with the back of his hand.

I've had too much sun, may still be drunk from the night before. Is that possible? I experience a glimmer of clairvoyance as convincing as the smell of exhaust. I close my eyes and the shape of the windshield floats on my eyelids, bright violet with a chartreuse trim. I know in an instant and without doubt that I will marry, never be good with plants, suffer incalculable loss that almost, almost tips me over, but I will right myself, I will forget Melody completely but she will show up and something about her as she is now — her straight defiant back in the rearview mirror — will be exactly the same. She'll give me a talisman and disappear as unexpectedly as she came.

Melody is still standing with her cigarette, holding one elbow. She's looking down the road, her back to us, the wind blowing a zigzag part in her hair. A faint patch of sweat on her pink shirt like a Rorschach test between her shoulder blades.

She finally drops the cigarette and crushes it with her sneaker. She walks toward the truck with her head bent down, climbs up beside me, and pulls the door shut. She doesn't even glance at the driver.

Skoochie over, she says. My arm touches the guy's bare arm and I feel the heat of his sunburn, a gliding muscle as he puts the truck in gear.

We all set, the guy asks.

We're ready, I say. There's a pine-tree air freshener, a pouch of tobacco on the dash, an apple slice to keep it fresh, smells as pristine as the South Pole. It's going to rain. Melody changes the radio station, hitting knots of static. The sky goes dark, darker, darker, and the first rumble is followed by a solid, thrilling crack. A blur of light low and pulsing. The rain tears into the pavement like a racing pack of whippets. Claws scrabbling over the top of the cab. Livid grey muscles of rain.

on the threshold

Melody and I are working on math in my dorm room. She kisses me on the mouth. Later, for the rest of my life, while washing dishes, jiggling drops of rain hanging on the points of every maple leaf in the window, or in a meeting when someone writes on a flowchart and the room fills with the smell of felt-tip marker — during those liminal non-moments fertile with emptiness — I will be overtaken by swift collages of memory. A heady disorientation, seared with pleasure, jarring. Among those memories: Melody's kiss. Because it was a kiss of revelatory beauty. I realized I had never initiated anything in my life. Melody acted; I was acted upon.

I'm not like that, I say, gay or anything.

She smiles, No big deal. She twists an auburn curl around in her finger, supremely unruffled. Aplomb. She's showing me how it's done.

I like you and everything, I say.

Relax, she says. She turns back to the math, engaging so quickly that she solves the problem at once.

⌁

What I feel on the side of the highway, ozone in the air, the epic sky: I am falling hugely in love. Hank, the guy who picked us up in his black truck. Brian Fiander. Melody, myself. Whomever. A hormonal metamorphosis, the unarticulated lust of a virgin as errant, piercing, and true as lightning. A half hour later the truck hydroplanes.

Hank slams on the brakes. The truck spins in two weight-less circles. I listen to the keening brakes of the eighteen wheeler coming toward us, ploughing a glorious wave of water in front of it. The sound as desperate and restrained as that of a whale exhausted in a net. I can see the grill of the eighteen wheeler's cab through the sloshing wave like a row of monster teeth. The transport truck stops close enough, our bumpers almost touching.

After a long wait, the transport driver steps down from the cab. He stands beside his truck, steely points of rain spiking off his shoulders like medieval armour. Melody opens her door and steps down. She walks toward the driver, but then she veers to the side of the road and throws up.

The driver of the transport truck catches up with her there. When Melody has finished puking he turns her toward him, resting his hands on her shoulders. She speaks and hangs her head. He begins to talk, admonishing, cajoling; once bending his head back and looking up into the rain. He chuckles. The thick film of water sloshing over the windshield makes their bodies wiggle like sun-drugged snakes. After a while he lifts her chin. He takes a handkerchief from an inside pocket and shakes it out and holds it at arm's length, examining both sides. He hands it to her and she wipes her face.

Hank whispers to me, I'm not responsible for this. He lays his hand on the horn.

Melody gets back in the truck. She's shivering. The other driver climbs into his cab. His headlights come on. The giant lights splinter into needles of pink and blue and violet and the rain is visible in the broad arms of light, and as the truck pulls out the lights dim and narrow, as if it has cunning. Then it drives away. Hank takes off his sunglasses and folds the arms and places them in a holder for sunglasses glued to the dash. He moves his hand over his face, down and up, and then he rests his forehead on the wheel. He holds the wheel tight.

What did you say to him, Hank asks. He waits for Melody to answer but she doesn't. Finally he lifts his head. He flings his arm over the back of the seat so he can turn the truck and I see the crackle of lines at the corners of his eyes.

⌒

I watch Melody inside the Irving station a couple of hours later, her pink sleeveless blouse through the window amid the reflections of the pumps and the black truck I'm leaning against. She passes through my reflection and, returning to the counter, passes through me again like a needle sewing something up. Hank opens the hood and pulls out the dipstick. He takes a piece of paper towel from his back pocket, draws it down the length of stick, stopping it from wavering.

Melody comes out with a bottle of orange juice. It has stopped raining. Steam lifts off the asphalt and floats into the trees. Sky, Canadian flag, child with red shirt — all mirrored in the glassy water on the pavement at our feet. A car passes and the child's reflection is a crazy red flame breaking apart under the tires. The juice in Melody's hand has an orange halo. A brief rainbow arcs over the wet forest behind the Irving station.

You married, Hank? Melody asks. He's still fiddling with things under the hood.

I believe I met you at the El Dorado, Melody says.

Hank unhooks the hood, lowers it, and lets it drop. He rubs his hands in the paper towel and gives her a look.

I don't think so, he says.

I believe you bought me a drink, Melody says.

You're most likely thinking of someone else, he says.

Could have sworn it was me, Melody says, it sure felt like me. She laughs and it comes out a honk.

I'm going to carry on by myself from here, Hank says.

But you're probably right, Melody says, the guy I'm thinking of wasn't wearing a ring.

Good luck, he says. Melody hefts herself up onto a stack of white plastic lawn chairs next to a row of barbeques and swings her legs. Hank gets in his truck and pulls out onto the highway.

I can take care of myself, Melody yells. But now we've lost

our ride, and it'll take a good hour to get to the clinic in
Corner Brook from here.

⌣

The nurse leans against the examining table with her arms
folded under her clipboard.

You'll need your mother's signature, she says. Anybody
under nineteen needs permission from a parent or guardian.
You'll need to sit before a board of psychiatrists in St. John's to
prove you're fit.

Tears slide fast to Melody's chin and she raises a shoulder
and rubs her face roughly against the collar of her jean jacket.

She wouldn't sign, Melody says.

The nurse turns from Melody and pulls a paper cone from
a dispenser and holds it under the water cooler. A giant wobbling bubble works its way up, breaking at the surface. It sounds
like a cooing pigeon, dank and maudlin. I can hear water rat-a-
tatting from a leaky eaves trough onto a metal garbage lid.

My mother has fourteen children, Melody says.

The nurse drinks the water and crunches the cup. She
presses the lever on the garbage bucket with her white shoe
and the lid smacks against the wall. She tosses the cup and it
hits the lid and falls inside. Then she wipes her forehead with
the back of her hand.

You can forge the signature and I'll witness it, she says. She
takes the top off the Bic pen with her teeth. She flicks a few
pages and shows Melody where to sign. Melody signs and the
nurse signs below.

I don't need to tell you, the nurse says.

I appreciate it, says Melody.

~

That year I live on submarine sandwiches microwaved in plastic wrap. When I peel back the wrap, the submarine hangs out soggy and spent, like a tongue after a strangling. The oozing processed cheese hot enough to raise blisters. I wear a lumber jacket over cheesecloth skirts, and red Converse sneakers. I learn to put a speck of white makeup in the outer corner of my eyes to give me an innocent, slightly astonished look. On Valentine's Day in the dorm elevator I tear an envelope; dried rose petals fall out and whirl in the updraft of the opening elevator doors and there is Brian Fiander. I see I was wrong; he isn't skinny. If he still wants me, he can have me. I will do whatever Brian Fiander wants and if he wants to dump me after, as he has Brenda Parsons, he can go right ahead. He seems to go through girls pretty quickly and I want to be gone through.

~

Melody and I get tickets on the CN bus into St. John's for the abortion. I wait for her outside a boardroom in the Health Sciences. I catch a glimpse of the psychiatrists, five men seated in a row behind a table. Melody comes out a half-hour later.

What did they say?

One of them commented on my hat, she says. He said I

must think myself pretty special with a fancy hat. He asked if I thought I was pretty special.

What did you say?

The same smile as when she kissed me. Learning to smile like that will take time. The rainbow must belong to some other story. Stretching over the hills behind the Irving station, barely there.

After the abortion I hold her hand. She's lying on a stretcher and she reaches a hand out over the white sheet that is tucked so tightly around her shoulders that she has to squirm to get her arm free.

Not too bad, she says. She is ashen. Tears from the corners of her eyes to her ears.

Sometimes you have to do things, she says.

⌣

During the rest of the winter I spend a lot of time with Wavy Fagan. She's marrying her high-school woodworking teacher; they have to keep the relationship secret. Wavy smokes, holding the cigarette out the window. I fan the fire alarm with her towel.

I don't spend much time with Melody; time together is exhausting. Wavy smokes, and she taps the window with her hard fingernail and tells me to come look. Six floors below, Melody is crossing the dark parking lot. It's snowing and a white circle of snow has gathered in the brim of her hat and it glows under the streetlight.

She's the one had the abortion for Hank Mercer, Wavy says.

— 2 —

I am drunk and in profound pain, my tooth. I am a forty-year-old widow in someone else's bed. Whose bed? Robert turns on the bedside light. Primrose Place is where I am. Robert's new house with new everything. Big housewarming party. I can feel the throb of it through the floorboards. Wrought iron this and marble that. Where I've woken up for the last eleven months. He untangles his bifocals from the lace doily on the side table and comes over to my side and gets down on his knees. He takes my cheeks in his hands. I can smell the alcohol in his sweat, on his breath.

Open up, he says.

I say, You have to take care of it.

It's five in the morning. He pays the taxi. I lean against the glass door of his office while he finds the keys. Everything behind the door leaps into its proper place just before the door swings open. The fluorescent lights flutter grey, then a bland spread of office light. The office simulates an office. A sterile environment for extracting a tooth. Robert passes down a hall of convincing office dividers. Turns on the X-ray machine.

That's got to warm up, he says.

Just pull it out, I say.

Robert gets a small card from the receptionist's desk and slings himself into a swivel chair. The chair rolls and tips and he is flung onto the floor. He grips the desk and drags himself up and sits in the chair. He puts a pen behind his ear and feels around on the desk for it and remembers it behind his ear. The top of his head shines damply.

Any allergies, abnormal medical conditions, sexually transmitted diseases? He's slurring. I don't bother.

He leaves the room and I hear water running in a sink. The rip rip rip of paper towels from a dispenser. He comes back and pulls on a pair of latex gloves, letting them snap at his wrists, flexing his fingers.

Who was the man you were talking to, Robert says.

The gloves are the smell I've noticed on his hands, like the smell of freshly watered geraniums. He takes an X-ray and leads me to the chair.

Make yourself comfortable, he says. There's a poster of rotting gums — enlarged, florid gums oozing pus, the roots of the blackened teeth exposed and bleeding. Photographs of everyone who works in the office, the other dentists, the dental hygienists, and receptionists. I look for the redhead. A brief, uncomplicated affair, he said, terrific sex. Long after it was over Robert tidied away her student loan and Visa. Braids and a lab coat covered in teddy bears and balloons. I sink into the chair and a moment later feel myself sink into the chair. Robert prepares a syringe. He drops it. He picks it up and looks at the tip. He scrutinizes the tip of the needle for some time.

That man was all over you, he says.

I'm allowed to have a conversation.

He tosses the syringe toward the garbage bucket; it hits the wall and bounces end over end across the room. Robert holds up one finger.

I'll get another one.

You do that, Robert. I can hardly open my mouth. He puts his hands on my face and leans in to look, his entire weight rests on my sore cheek. He steadies himself and straightens up.

The infection is too severe, he says.

Coward, I say.

We should run a course of antibiotics first.

Robert, please.

This is unethical, he says, I love you. He begins to sob. He sobs silently with his mouth hanging open, his shoulders curled in, cradling himself. I don't care what position I've put him in. His house with the new, leakless skylights and cedar sauna. The spacious greenhouse, pong of aggressive rose bushes, dill, peat. Asking his dinner guests to pull the pearl onions from the earth. Orchids in aquariums with timed sprinklers. Philip Glass on the sound system, building tense, cerebral crescendos. Density of pixels this, lightweight that, gigs of this, surround sound. Pull my fucking tooth, you drunken idiot.

You are so remote, he says, wiping his eyes.

If you're crying about that guy.

Don't you feel anything?

He sticks the needle into my infected gum and I dig my nails into his wrist and my heel kicks the chair. The numbing spreads up my face and partway across my upper lip. My cheek is cold and stupid and the pain is gone in less than a minute. My nails break his skin.

We'll wait until you're good and frozen, he says. He leaves the room. I hear him walk into the reception area. He crashes into something. A coffee maker starts to grumble. The smell of coffee. He turns on a radio. A woman says, That's the reality of the situation, then static and classical music. He returns with the X-ray. He seems to have sobered.

The bacteria think they died and went to heaven, he says. He has become reverent.

Robert, I need to know you'll stop if I ask you to. He clips the X-ray to a light board. My teeth look blue and ghostly. The white jawbone. I think of my husband buried in the cemetery near Quidi Vidi Lake. Robert goes into the reception area, I hear him pour a coffee. He opens a filing cabinet drawer.

He shouts, Are you good and frozen?

⌒

The toothache had been mild for weeks. I think I'm awake but the bed is facing in the wrong direction. Or I'm in the wrong bed. A toilet bowl filling continuously. Wet leaves and earth, is there a window? Stenographers on squeaky keyboards wait for a breath of wind and resume. A car unzips a skim of water. Hard fingernails clicking glass, the leaves, the skylight, keying data. Data dripping from leaf tip to leaf tip. A religious cult in the sewer can be overheard whispering in the toilet bowl. A conspiracy and the stenographers ache to crack it. Wind sloshes through the trees and the typing subsides. The trees are just trees. I am my tooth, a monolithic grief. A man beside me. Please be Des; please. It is Des.

The beach to ourselves, the park closed, early September.

What heat, so late in the season. Each wave leaves a ribbon of glare in the sand as it withdraws. The sun is low and red, scissored by the long grass. Des strips to his underwear, trots toward the water. Stands at the edge of the ocean. High up, a white gull.

Des charges, arms raised over his head, yelling. The gull is silent. So high up it's barely there. Wide circles. It dips closer. The wave's crest tinged pink, fumbling forward. He dives through the falling crest. The soles of his feet. He passes through, bobs on the other side. Flicks water from his hair. His fist flies up, wing of water under his arm. The gull screeches. Metallic squawk, claws outstretched, reaching for the sand. The sun through the grass on the hill laserbeams the gull's eye, a red holograph. The gull's pupil is a long midnight corridor to some prehistoric crimson flash deep in the skull.

He calls, Water's great. My shirt, jeans, one sock stretches long. I have to hop. The sock gives up. I run hard. The wave is building beneath the bed. Except how cold. My body seizes.

Look at the one coming, Des says. The wave comes with operatic silence. Such surety, self-knowledge, so cold and meaningless and full of blasé might. I reach out my hand. Here it comes. A wave full of light, nearly transparent, lacy webbing on the underside. The ocean sucking hard on my spine. The sandy bottom drops away.

It smashes us. The bed plummets and thumps the floor. The room makes itself felt. Dresser, a housecoat on a hook. Des died four years ago of heart failure. Peanut butter jar on the floor, fridge open. Holding the knife. Smoking toast in the stuck toaster. The red light of the ambulance on the walls of the hall-way. Now I'm awake.

～

Tequila I drank, scotch. Elasticky top and sarong. Beer. Robert warned me, when he throws a party. Dancing. Slamming doors, laughter, the Stones. I have dated, since Des died, no one: an air traffic controller, a very young painter, no one, the reporter guy, absolutely no one, the carpenter. The tooth became unbearable two days ago. I didn't tell Robert. Pleased to meet you, hope you guess my name. You can't leave. How can you leave? Bodies pressed close, smoky ceiling. Blow the speakers. We took a cab. Hope you guess my. Get a taxi. If we dance. In the fridge door. Mine are the cold ones. Pleased to meet you. Have one of mine. The cold ones. I got laid. Tell me. I'll tell you after this. We need a toast. Our coats are where? Forget the coats. Don't leave, it's a party. Because the toilet. What hap-pened to the tequila? Your own stupid fault. My wife took the traditional route. Does it have a worm in it? I'll put one in if you like. There have been women, yes. There have been women, I'll admit. We'll call ourselves the Fleshettes. The peo-ple impressed me most. I'm not responsible. Hope you guess my. We haven't talked. We're talking now. This is talking? Name. I love you. Don't say that. I love you, what do you think? I think more beer.

～

The sky is the deepest blue it gets before it begins to look black. The stars are blue. The trees roar with wind and become quiet. I lie flat on my husband's grave and look at the stars. Freshly mowed grass, a faint marshy smell, the ducks at the edge of the lake. This morning, resting my head against the hand dryer in the bathroom of Robert's office. Tears start this way: the bridge of my nose, my eyelids, the whole face tingling, the clutch of a muscle in the throat. The smell of burnt coffee — homey, unloved office coffee — makes me cry. Some songs: Patsy Cline. Bad blue icing on the birthday cake the girls bought for the boss. I cry at least four times a day. The tears catch in the plastic rims of my glasses. My eyelids like slugs. While waiting for the elevator I hear laughter inside, ascending, inclusive, sexual. I cry with jealousy. Marcy Andrews coming into the bathroom after me. Unclicking her purse, getting the cotton swab out of a pill bottle, tapping two pills into my hand. Marcy smoothing her thumbs over my wet cheeks. She turns me to the mirror and she looks hard at me.

She says, Lipstick will give you a whole new lease.

I can't be alone, I say.

The leaves in the graveyard smell leathery, pumpkinish. The branches creak when the wind rubs them together. Des's hands folded over a rose, his wedding ring. When do the teeth fall away from the skull? Does that happen? It's beginning to get cold. Snow on his headstone makes me panicky.

A flashlight waves erratically through the shrubs, catching the bright green moss on a carved angel's cheek, her cracked wing. Another flashlight, soft oval bouncing in the leaves overhead, scuffle of feet. I'm surrounded by a circle of teenagers with baseball bats and fence pickets. They step, one by one, out of the trees and bushes. Or else they have always been standing there. All the headstones, tipping, lichen-crusted. I stand up, my legs watery. We stand like that, not speaking or moving.

You seen a guy run through here?

I whisper, No. I haven't seen anybody. Three policemen arrive and the teenagers flee. A policeman steps forward and puts an arm around my shoulder and I cry into his armpit.

⌒

Robert lowers a tool into my mouth and I say, Stop.

I say, That was a test.

He says, That was a scalpel. I would just trust me if I were you.

I feel him cut the gum and fold the flesh back. His eyes full of veins blue and violet; my blood sprays dots on his glasses. He takes up another instrument and tugs at the tooth, twisting it, and I feel it tearing away. The hoarse, sputtering noise of the suction hose removing blood and saliva. Robert worked for nothing in Nicaragua after he graduated, teaching the revolutionaries to be dentists, the distant spitting of gunfire in the fields beyond his classroom. During the dot-com boom he invested — in and out — unspeakably rich.

My tooth hits a chrome bowl with a bright ping. He begins to sew the stitches. I feel the thread move through the gum and the sensation, though painless, nauseates me. Three tight stitches, the side of my mouth puckered. He gives me a wad of cotton and tells me to bite down. He peels the latex gloves. I worry the loose ends of the stitches with my wooden tongue. They feel like cat whiskers.

I've wanted to ask for some weeks, Robert says.

Maybe this is not the best time, I say.

I want to marry you, he says.

⌒

The sound of the sliding metal rings when I rip open the shower curtain unnerves me. Waiting for the toaster to pop, a butter knife in my hand, I am aware of a presence. The washer shimmies across the laundry room floor until it works the plug from the wall and the motor goes quiet. The water stops slushing. An engrossing, animated silence. Every object — the vacuum cleaner, a vase of dried thistles — has become sensitive. The fridge knows. The unmade bed is not ordinary. I put a glass down and check. It's exactly where I set it down. Loving a dead person takes immense energy and it is making me cry.

⌒

Robert works the champagne cork with his thumbs. The cork bounces off the ceiling and hits a mirror, causing a web of cracks. He hands me my glass and I can feel the fizz on my face.

He says, This is the happiest day of my life.

We twine arms and drink and the awkward intimacy of this, the complete lack of irony — I know instantly I've made a mistake.

⌒

Robert is still at work and I'm watching the decorating channel. The camera slowly roves through a palatial, empty house in Vermont, a woman's chipper voice: Here we have an oak table, very countryish, but *workable* chairs, this dining room absolutely screams to be used. Use me, it's screaming!

I turn the TV off and listen to the shrill nothing that fills Robert's house. Leaves swirl off the lawn in twisting columns. A brown leaf hits the glass and sticks. The starlings are flying in formation over the university. A black cloud draws together and becomes thin as it changes direction. The sky is full of grey luster and the starlings seem feverish. I remember Des parking by the university once, just to watch them. It was late, we had groceries, ice cream in the trunk.

They're just playing, he said. I want to stay here, don't you? I want to watch all night.

I think: If you are there, get in touch with me now. I believe suddenly that he can, that it is just a matter of my asking.

The phone rings at exactly that instant. It rings and rings and rings. Then it stops. I put my hand on the receiver and I can feel a warm thrum. Then it rings again, loud. I go upstairs and brush my teeth. I rinse and start flossing. The phone rings again. It's ringing in all the rooms, terrifying me. I pour a bath and get in, and when it's deep enough I dunk my ears under the water.

⌒

Robert gives me a glass of scotch and drops into the chair beside me. He presses his watch face so the dial glows, sending a circle of green light zigzagging across his face. The sale of my house has come through. A young couple with a dalmatian. Most of the furnishings went to the Sally Ann. A closet full of Des's shirts, a key ring with a plastic telescope, inside which there is a picture of Des and me on vacation in Mexico. It has to be held to a light. We are laughing, drinking from coconut shells. I'd let all the plants die. Robert has everything we need.

You're tired, I say, we're both tired.

What do you think of stem cell research, he says.

There are the dishes.

I could take a hair out of your head and make another you.

The laundry is —

Two of you. The real you and another you.

I know I'm tired.

One you is a roomful already.

I can't have sex with you tonight if that's what you're thinking, I say.

Why would I be thinking a thing like that?

I'm drifting to sleep while he talks. I dream I say I want my real husband, and I don't know if I've spoken out loud or not. I believe that Des is in the chair beside me and things are as they were five years ago, as if the past can do that. Lay itself down on the present. Cover it over. Become the present, even briefly. A pair of flip-flops, I'd stumbled and skinned my toe. Des had been hammering all day. The hammering had stopped, but the silent ringing of the hammer went on. It was late September and we went to the beach.

⌣

In the morning I hear a car coming up the long driveway and I leap out of bed. A dark green minivan pulls up under the trees. The windshield is opaque with the shadows of the maple trees. The van parks and a man steps out. He's wearing cream-coloured pants and a pastel plaid shirt. He stretches and puts his hands on his hips. He helps a little girl out of the driver's side. She's wearing a white cotton dress and the skirt bells with the breeze. Finally the passenger door opens and a woman gets out. I'm standing in the upstairs window, struggling to get my jeans on. There is a wave rising inside me. It's full of light. It's dull and smart and hurting my throat. Robert rolls over in bed.

He says, Who would disturb us at this hour?

The woman has her hand over her eyes to block the sun and she's looking up into the bedroom window where I'm standing and I know it's Melody without even recognizing her. I run down the stairs and out the back without my shoes. I have never initiated anything in my life. I forgot her completely and here she is. She'll give me something.

She's exactly the same. The child is just like her. The guy

holds out his hand. Melody says his name and I tell him I'm thrilled, but I forget his name. I forget the child's name but it's Jill.

I tried to call, she says, holding out her arms.

I say, I'm married. I start to cry. Melody kisses me.

I whisper, I've messed up, Melody.

She says, You'll just have to do something about it.

Mouths, Open

A woman climbs over me for the window seat — hair like vanilla ice cream, a purple mink. Beneath the fur, a sweatsuit and spanking new sneakers. She's got a paper bag with twine handles. Lingerie. Her fingernails are false and black, an inch and a half.

You raise your eyes from your book. She tears a hot pretzel — the bread inside porous and steaming — and dips it into the tiny container of honey mustard. The dexterity of a lobster. After each bite she touches her nails against a napkin, rubbing carefully under the concave side. A glistening gob of green gum on the side of her plate, the teeth marks. She's a sex worker who flies to Halifax from St. John's for the weekend. What costs as much as a blow job, a carton of red peppers? Sable earmuffs?

We are in Cuba. The lawn sprinkler beside the pool whispering rounds of silver ammunition that pock the sand. A

*born one
sex but feel
inclined to be
the opposite
sex*

cockroach with an indigo shell. Banana leaves as sharp as switchblades. The plastic of my recliner sweating against my cheek. The pool looks as solid as a bowl of Jell-O, a jar of Dippity-Do. The Italian transsexuals lower their bodies until they are submerged to the neck, careful of their curls. They have the most beautiful nipples. I can't take my eyes off their more-than-perfect breasts.

At the kitchen table at home in St. John's. The tablecloth is gone; the table is red, bright red enamel paint, and there is the creamer, full of milk. The kitchen is pumpkin, forest green cupboards. The kitchen screams. My hands are on the table in front of me. I want to throw the creamer. Milk fluttering over your head, a long ribbon of surrender. It is a huge effort not to give in and throw it. Then my fist slams.

What is wrong with you, I shout.

I say, Speak. Do you think I'm joking?

You say, I'm afraid of you.

This is the first thing you've said. There have been pauses. I keep thinking, What is my tone? I vary my tone. We already know the lines. Do you think I'm joking? (whisper) Speak! (shout) What the fuck is wrong with you? (monotone) Do I exist? Maybe I don't exist. (giggles)

But it's reassuring that you're afraid of me. I have been worried that I don't exist. I don't think I am, therefore.

Just speak. Speak.

You say, I'm thinking of leaving you.

The beach, in a windstorm. I bang my toe on a concrete block emerging from the sand. Pass a demolished building. A giant slab of concrete with a painted silhouette of Che Guevara excavated from the ruins. I stand on tippy-toe and put my mouth up to his giant lips, posing for a photograph. Weeping, sand under my contact lens, scratching my eye. The wind flicks the tail of my dress against the concrete slab like a propeller trying to turn over, resolutely stalled. Everything in Cuba is at a standstill, waiting for ignition. Because of the embargo there is no anaesthetic for operations — everybody pre-operative, prepped. You wave me out of the picture.

You say, Just Che. By himself.

In the Museum of the Revolution in Havana, a clear plastic Petri dish containing a sample of Che Guevara's hair and a sample of his beard. I feel ashamed for pretending to kiss him. Che and Fidel, wax figures, beating their way through the plastic bushes. The glass eyeballs have a yellowish cast. Beads of clear varnish on their foreheads, cheeks. Mouths open, as if they are shouting to soldiers behind them, or gasping for breath. We are here for a conference. You're talking about the revolutionary spirit of Gian-Lorenzo Bernini, the seventeenth-century sculptor.

We go into another hotel during the downpour, for espresso.

You say, Someone else is doing the . . .

You lift your chin toward an open doorway farther down

the lobby. A couple is dancing. The patio is a slick of wet slate, and the reflections of a red skirt and the shadows of the palm trees are hydroplaning at their feet. Clothes soaked to the skin. A black man teaching a white woman the tango. A black girl carries a giant armload of canary yellow towels, brilliant against her black, black cheek. She slits her eyes at them. Everything is a ripe pomegranate. *fruit w tough orange skin w segments of sweet red gelatinous flesh*

I say, Should we be sleeping together? If you're leaving me?

You say, I don't see why not.

Lightning cracks low over the horizon, stunted like bonsai trees. The espresso is strong. Tiny cups. The chink of the cup in the saucer.

I say, From now on, if I say I love you, I'm speaking out of habit.

I wonder, what are you? Am I you? What don't I love anymore?

Outside, we hold our feet under a fountain that squirts from a stone fish. I watch you hold up your foot. You turn it and the sand peels away from your ankle. I love your foot. That is the only part of you I still love.

I say, I'm going to think of you as a long series of gestures. You are your nose and eyes and mouth and the things you do with them.

You say, Don't forget my cock.

The hotel room smells of a lemon venom: insecticide. You are asleep. I stand on the bed and photograph you. Your arms thrown over your head, warding off the blades of sunlight from the swinging louvered shutters, a fencing match on your naked back. The maid has twisted the white towels into the shape of swans. Two towel swans joined at the beak, as if kissing.

Back in the kitchen, at home, the creamer stops pulsing. The creamer has lost meaning.

I say, This marriage can be anything you want.

You say, I might be happier without you in my life.

I say, Let's go somewhere. We need a change.

I guess I should read the *Manifesto*. The literary critic who spoke before you at the conference said it is an authorless tract. That Marx repeatedly tried to make it sound as though it came from thin air, or rose by itself from the people, spontaneously. He was willing to claim the bad poetry of his youth that even Penguin didn't want to publish. But the *Manifesto* just was. Just passed through his pen.

Tell me what happened? Did you meet somebody?

The simultaneous translator becomes exhausted late afternoon, breaking down, translating word by word instead of for the sense. So each word is encased in explosive consonants, the meaning picked up later like shattered bullet casings. She is staccato, and then stuck. The people's . . . ? The people's . . . ? She looks around the room hopelessly. Someone offers the word *struggle*. Ah, yes, The people's struggle. The room explodes with laughter.

In the pastry shop. A young black girl with long black braids, thousands, in a ponytail on the top of her head. Like squirts of oil from a squeeze bottle, shiny, dragonfly blue in the light. She wears a slippery Lycra body suit. It stretches over her breasts and bum like burst bubblegum, bright pink. She gets in line next to you. Her hip presses into the glass of the display case.

There is an older woman with a cane. We are both waiting, this older woman and I. The heat — there must be a lot of ovens — they keep bringing out bread tied in knots and other shapes. Giant wicker baskets of oily golden sailor's knots. A man stacks them on steel shelves — the girl is talking to you, she is digging a high heel into the tiles and rocking a little. She has full breasts and is very young. She may be sixteen. But she may be younger.

She may be the age of your daughter, fifteen. The girl touches your collar. You are blushing darkly. But you are laughing too. Two sides of the same coin, shame and pleasure.

There is more bread and a blast of heat. You are buying the girl pastries. She is laughing and pointing and the woman behind the counter puts what the girl wants into a white box. The girl hesitates before she points to each pastry. She looks coyly at you each time she touches the glass with her finger, and each time you nod.

But you have become serious now. The girl turns and sees me. Something passes over her face, perhaps embarrassment. This is what I feel: Fuck off, bitch. But the girl is only the age of my stepdaughter, whom I love and protect. I am ashamed of the look on my face. The woman with the cane is joined by her friend. They speak a few words to each other and leave.

A moment more, and the woman with the cane returns. She asks: Do you understand Spanish?

I say no.

She says, A little?

A little, I say. This isn't true. What I understand is less than a little, but I know what she will say. She points to her eye and then out — so that I know to look out.

She is telling me to look out. Her hand grips the plastic handle of the cane tightly. She does not hesitate or pause as she speaks. She isn't experimenting with tone. She is telling me, Yes, he was flattered. Don't doubt it. He was flattered.

All I want is to be away from her, for your sake. But I am moved that she has come back into the pastry shop to tell me. She says, AIDS. I hear it mingled with the Spanish.

Then she leaves.

There is a white statue of a woman with a basket on her shoulder at the end of the pool. Bernini talked about the paleness of marble. The absence of flesh tone makes it difficult to capture likeness. Would you recognize someone who had poured a bag of flour over his head? To compensate, Bernini suggests drawing the face just as it is about to speak, or after it has just spoken. That's when the face is most characteristic of itself. He's responsible for the sixteenth-century fashion of portraits with the lips parted. We are most ourselves when we are changing.

I say, We can change certain things.

It's not that.

We can sleep with other people. Is that what you want?

You say you are making up your mind. You're sorry. You can't explain. It's as much a mystery for you as it is for me.

The man who lends towels and novels is set up in a grass hut with an impaled and glazed blowfish. This man leans on his elbows, chin in hands, and watches the transsexuals. They seem to let their mouths hang open, in a kind of pout. Like inflated dolls that are ready-made for oral sex.

Before me my cup is very white and the white saucer is on the white table. Espresso. The table shimmers in its whiteness. A fly lands on the rim of the cup. The fly is so blue-black that it makes me think: significance. There is significance here. What is it?

The fly touches the cup, and the whiteness of the cup becomes whiter.

You say, You look insane.

You say this just as I am applying significance to the white cup.

How did you know?

In the evening we meet Carl, Jorge, and Johann, from Austria. Carl takes a switchblade from the pocket over his calf. He opens it with an elegant motion of his wrist. There is a bartender working over a pestle and mortar several yards away.

Carl says, You want me to demonstrate? He raises his chin toward the bartender. I see the blade open the white shirt and blood flushing. Carl closes the knife and slides it back into his pocket.

Jorge is studying to be a veterinarian. He picks up the cat that rubs against his leg. The tail under his nose.

Carl says, No animal can pass him without he picks it up.

Johann: And they could kill him; he is allergic.

I carry a pill, says Jorge, or I die like this. He holds the cat's tail in his teeth.

I say, Will you work with big animals or small?

He leans forward. We have finished four bottles of rum and two, no three, rounds of beer.

He says, I want to work in an abattoir. I don't know how you say in English.

slaughter house

I say, But they kill animals there. I thought you loved animals?

These cats will kill him, says Johann, if they break his skin.

Jorge says, It's a simple operation, the gun they put to the head like that. He holds the flashlight to my temple and flicks the light so my cheek glows orange.

And it scrambles the brain, says Jorge, switching off the flashlight. He sits back and his wicker chair screeches unexpectedly. His throat is exposed by a floodlight in a palm tree. It's covered with bruises like squashed blueberries, hickeys. I realize he is much younger than me.

Jorge tosses the flashlight to you. It turns over in the air and lands in your hand with a neat smack.

He says, Why don't you put this in your wife's pussy tonight? Is big enough?

Everybody laughs uneasily, and Carl changes the subject.

I think: This afternoon I saw one of the transsexuals rest her feet on Jorge's thigh. He cupped her feet in his hand. Her feet were strong and nicely shaped, like meat-eating flowers. I imagine again Carl's switchblade opening the bartender. The bartender may finally get a rest. He's been here since eight in the morning. The transsexuals are both very tall, with high cheekbones and beautiful breasts. The nipples are beautiful. They have changed so much. Full lips. Comic-book eyes. Betty Boop. They go topless at poolside. I've seen one of them riding down the beach at sunset on a bay horse. A loop of reins slapping on both sides of the withers. Sand tossed. You, a long way from shore, you stand. There is a sandbar, and the ocean comes to your knees. One of the transsexuals turns a Sea-Doo sharply, so a white curtain of surf falls on your shoulders like an ermine mantle.

I shaved your neck before we left St. John's. Shaving cream like a neck brace holding you, a guillotine. The scrudge of the razor against your neck and hair, and cream piling. You were kneeling, and you turned and pressed your face into my skirt. Smearing chiffon like a hand wiping condensation from a window.

I realize I am at a table with four men and a flashlight. I laugh. The rum is like a time-lapse film playing in my skin. Briefly, I feel a leaden euphoria. I am most myself now.

We have been given the key to a different hotel room after checkout so we can shower before the long trip home. The room is more luxurious. It is dark, all the curtains drawn, and we turn on a light. We have to shower quickly to catch the bus to the airport. There is a dresser with a giant mirror.

I say, There isn't time.

My breasts flour white where the bikini covered me.

One foot on the bed frame and the heel of my hand on the desk edge. You stand behind me, gripping my hipbones, the strength in your thighs lifting me off my feet, letting me touch down. I watch in the mirror. Your hair is long and wet, stuck to tanned skin. Mouths open. I love you.

In the bathroom you open a jar of coconut pomade and put some in your hair. Pomade that someone has left behind. Another traveller. Later, in the Halifax airport, we sleep on benches, waiting for our connecting plane. I sleep and feel the planes taking off through the vibrations in the vinyl couch. I smell through every dream the coconut pomade. You smell like someone else.

The Way the Light Is

Mina O'Leary pulls a long silver skirt from her cupboard and holds it to her waist, one hand sweeping the folds. The fabric falls in sharp pleats, the light from the bedside lamp flashing in it.

How about this?

You sure have beautiful things.

It's stuff. I just like *stuff*.

The price tag still dangling from the waistband. Dried roses, petals crusty, in a vase on the vanity. I focus on the roses, but they look inert. The lack of motion in the dead roses buzzes. She picks a pair of nylons off the floor.

I'll put these on, I'd be wearing them in real life.

She takes armloads of clothes off the bed and throws them in the closet. She stretches the white duvet over the crumpled sheets.

Mina: I'm doing this mainly so you can watch me move.

Me: Put on that gold coat and give it a flap. Like the wings of the insect.

Mina: Okay, cool.

I'm making a five-minute film based on a poem by John Steffler, "The Green Insect." The poem is about the *elusive*. I want to shoot a combination of animation and live footage. I need a woman who looks like a grasshopper. A woman who will sit in a white wicker chair with her ankles drawn up near her bum, knees sticking out. A woman who doesn't get kinks in her neck. The insect doesn't have to be a woman. It could be almost anything you follow because you can't help yourself. It could be a chiffon scarf floating down Duckworth Street in the wind. I saw a beautiful Chinese film with a recurring shot of a long, almost transparent scarf tangled in some branches at dusk. But I like faces. French movies always take a long time with a face. The plot turns when a man raises an eyebrow. Bergman spends a long time on a face, but there is no plot.

What could capture the essence of this poem. No single image by itself, but a storm of images. Some children with sparklers running down the sidewalk at dusk. Bannerman Park with Christmas lights. The insect is anything there's no holding on to. And greenness. Something you ache to own.

My eight-year-old daughter in a purple bathing suit, swinging in the hammock Mina brought back from France last summer. We are around the bay, my daughter is reading a book, and I'm watching her from an upstairs window. She's completely absorbed in the pleasure of reading, the warmth of the sun, the long grass brushing her back with each sway of the low-slung hammock. Finally she gets up and wanders onto the dirt lane in front of the house. Her feet are bare. She's been wearing that bathing suit all summer, sleeping in it, picking blackberries that stain her teeth, leaping off a boulder into the river. Her long hair in a loose ponytail. She throws a baton. Far up in the blue sky it becomes liquid, a rope of mercury, but it comes down fast, bouncing off the pavement on its white rubber ends. There's no way to keep this moment in the present.

INT. RAMSHACKLE SUMMER HOUSE - DAY

MINA stands at a window on the second floor of
a weathered saltbox. The glass is old and
warped. She's watching a child in the long
grass throwing a baton. Her HUSBAND enters
and stands behind her. He's wearing swimming
trunks, his body is wet. She tilts her head
and he kisses her neck. He unbuttons her
blouse so it falls off her shoulders. Lowers
her bra strap.

          MINA
    She can see us.

          HUSBAND
    She can't. The way the light is.

Mina closes her eyes for a moment, lets her
husband touch her breasts. Then, tentatively,
she waves to the child on the lawn. The child
waves back.

I want Mina O'Leary riding the bus in St. John's in a rain-
storm. She's in the back, a blur of green moving toward the
door. She gets off and snaps open a green umbrella. Droplets of
rain spring away from the tight silk. The air brakes sigh, steam
rises from the pavement. The umbrella tips over her head.
Drops hang, jiggling, from the steel points of the umbrella's
skeleton. Her face, *thinking*. Liv Ullman is always thinking, her
face is young, young, young. They just talk, Bergman's actors,
straight into the camera about humiliation, fear of the dark,
death. Liv Ullman strikes a match and lights the lantern, a glow
floods up from the wooden table to her chin. They are always
on an island. There are vampires, sacrificed lambs. A crow with
a giant beak. Bodies draped in white sheets lying on slabs of
stone, desolate fields of snow seeping into the mud. Trudging, a
lot of trudging. Then, like a jewel, a flashing ruby dropped in
a bucket of tar, Bergman offers a bowl of strawberries, or a
child. A greenish cast over Mina O'Leary's cheeks from the
streetlight through the silk umbrella.

INT. AN ABSTRACT SPACE - DAY

Mina is twenty-seven, she has dark, shiny
hair that she tucks behind her ears, a severe

cut that's growing out with deliberate
dishevelment. When she's listening she
becomes very still, captivated.

> MINA
> My mother was young, she was twenty-
> one when she had me, and I was the
> fourth. My father was away.

> YOUNG WOMAN
> Where was your father?

> MINA
> Oh, fucking around I guess.
> (laughs)
> . . . no, my father drank and he was
> a musician, so that was part of it.

She reaches for a lobster claw from a platter
in front of her, cracks it open with a hammer. She's eating the meat with her fingers;
such intent pleasure, both aloof and sensu-
ous, unwittingly intimate.

> MINA
> He'd get these houses for us on the
> outskirts of town, isolated, and she'd
> have to wait for him, just wait . . .

                    YOUNG WOMAN
To bring her food and stuff?

                    MINA
To get her out of there. She'd wait
and wait, and he just wouldn't come.
I think she went kind of crazy. She
saw things . . .

                    YOUNG WOMAN
What kind of things?

                    MINA
Scary things.

                    YOUNG WOMAN
Like what though?

                    MINA
Well, like once —

                    YOUNG WOMAN
No wait, don't tell me if it's too
scary.

                    MINA
No, it's nothing, she saw a dog,

```
that's all, a dog on the lawn pacing
back and forth, waiting to get in.
```

The John Steffler poem says that after the insect was trapped it tore up history. "It ripped up reality, it flung away time and space / I couldn't believe the strength it had, / it unwound its history, ran out its spring in kicks and / rage, denied itself, denied me and my ownership."

There's a dried squirt of breast milk on my computer screen. I wipe it away with the tip of my finger and saliva, the pixels magnified in the wet streak. The way my husband, Jason, talks to our new son: Oh, the saucy thing, the *saucy* thing. Jason can't get enough of him.

Mina will be here soon, I say.

She'll eat him up, Jason says.

Mina, in Paris, about to miss her flight home for Christmas. She has to find an elevator, a moving sidewalk underground, swinging doors on the left. Forget *that*. She drags the luggage cart outside and crosses the four-lane highway between the two wings of the airport.

```
EXT. AIRPORT RUNWAY - DAY
```

```
A plane is taxiing away from Mina, who is
running through a blizzard. She stops and
waves her red wallet over her head. The plane
```

```
stops like a sluggish animal, a crocodile,
the staircase falling open like a jaw. The
attendant steps out into the snow in a short-
sleeved white blouse and navy skirt.
```

Bergman has said about writing a script, "All in all, split-second impressions that disappear as quickly as they come, forming a brightly colored thread sticking out of the dark sack of the unconscious. If I wind up this thread carefully a complete film will emerge, brought out with pulse-beats and rhythms characteristic of just this film." I think about how so much of a good story seems to happen elsewhere, off the canvas or screen or page, in Europe or a backwater New Brunswick town, in what is left unsaid. A word on the tip of the tongue, ungraspable. The teasing smush of a feather boa over naked breasts in a striptease. Mina is ten years younger than me, and is rarely jealous of her husband, Yvonique. It's New Year's Eve, a dinner party at Mina's. Her necklace has broken and she's trying to fix it.

Mina: I can't believe this. Can you believe this? I loved this necklace.

Yvonique asks the baby, Do you know what Coco Chanel says? When you walk into a room, *think* champagne, *feel* champagne, *be* champagne. But of course, you will be carried into the room. The same rules apply.

He talks to the infant with an ease that suggests an affinity between them I can't imitate. Anything I say to the baby sounds studied or, when I'm overwhelmed by the fact of him, maudlin. Yvonique rips a bottle of champagne from an ice

THE WAY THE LIGHT IS

bucket and tells us one judges the quality by the size of the bubbles (the tinier the better) and their plenitude. They must taste crisp and clean.

I think *plenitude* is one of those words that only gets spoken by someone whose native tongue isn't English. I want to say this, but I'm afraid of offending him. Yvonique becomes shy at unpredictable moments, blushing dark red, his earlobes the darkest, his gold earring seeming to brighten.

Jason says, Can you taste a bubble?

Yvonique: Oui. But of course.

He reaches over the fireplace for a machete, which he unsheathes from a tooled leather case hanging by a gold braid and tassel. He places the bottle on its side with the neck sticking over the edge of the dining table and runs the blade of the machete around the glass so it whistles eerily.

Mina: He's bluffing, he doesn't know how to do that!

Yvonique lifts the bottle and cleanly slices the glass with the machete so champagne gushes over his upturned face and open mouth for a moment before he fills the crystal flutes on the sideboard. We have finished the second course and there is a pause.

In the kitchen Mina has thrown out Yvonique's roux. We hear a spat of bitter words.

She says, But I thought you were done with it.

Jason and I sit at the table waiting for the main course. The other guests have left the table to smoke. The baby is nursing. We sit for a long time in the empty room.

Jason says, What colour are these walls?

Wedgwood blue, I say.

Someone in another part of the house turns on some music. Apocalyptica — *Plays Metallica by Four Cellos* — so loud that the ornaments on the Christmas tree vibrate. Then it's turned down, and then off. The whole house is silent. Outside, the city is covered in a quick, brief snowfall.

Jason says, Maybe we should order out.

Yvonique kicks the swinging door open, holding a platter of lamb studded with wizened apricots. We eat and exclaim how good it is, but afterward Yvonique seems disappointed. He says, Has nobody noticed the flavour of green tea?

The dessert arrives with a young Australian woman: a President's Choice tiramisu with a tartan ribbon around the rim.

I want to catch the dessert on fire, says Mina, all season I've been lighting desserts on fire.

I ask the Australian what she does.

I can't tell you, it sounds too pretentious.

Oh, go ahead.

I'm a digital artist.

INT. DOWNTOWN CAFÉ - DAY

Mina is sitting in a fat armchair near the window looking out onto Water Street. She is speaking to her girlfriend. The waitress brings them lattes in tall glasses with long spoons. It's lunchtime, and at first Mina is distracted by the passing lawyers and teenagers.

MINA

Do you know what Yvonique said, that
he developed my palate. Can you
believe that?

YOUNG WOMAN

He roasts a mean duck.

MINA

Like I'm trailer trash.
   (giggles)
It's true.

YOUNG WOMAN

Me too. I'm trailer trash too.

MINA

Lay it here, sister.
   (they slap hands in the air)

YOUNG WOMAN

But don't you love him?

MINA

We were both coming out of heavy
relationships and we agreed not to
get emotionally involved. But the
sex was so good. So good. We just

kept going like that, a month, two
months. This was Paris. Then I told
him I cared if he slept with someone
else.

We hear Mina's voice while watching her run
through a sparse birch forest. She's wearing
a white cotton dress and white sneakers, she
is running very fast. Her feet hardly touching the ground, sunlight crashing through the
overhead branches, she is just a blur.

        MINA (V.O.)
That's what we agreed we'd say if we
found ourselves getting emotionally
involved. I care if you sleep with
someone else. And he said, *run*. Just
that one word, *run*. I wrote it on a
piece of paper in big block letters
with a highlighter at work. RUN. I
just stared at the word. I kept it
on my desk for a long time. It would
turn up under a pile of books. It
was my father all over again.

After midnight on New Year's Eve the digital artist and
Yvonique got lost in the crowd on the waterfront. They fell
into a snowbank together, kissing.

Everyone did ecstasy, Mina says, it happens.

And that doesn't bother you, I ask.

She's sucking the last bit of meat from a lobster claw.

Not *really*. She thinks for a minute, wipes her lips with the back of her hand. I mean, if it *meant something* I guess it would bother me. *I guess* it would bother me if it meant something. I'm not sure.

Jason and I sit with the car warming up in the parking lot of the Avalon Mall, Cuban music on the radio. I think of a tropical ravine we passed once, in a tourist bus, and a band that came out and played at a dusty bus stop at ten o'clock in the morning, an hour outside Havana. There was a corrugated roof of green plastic and the musicians wore white straw hats and white pants that looked green under the shelter. Jason bought an orange. How charged the musicians were. I had licked a drop of orange juice before it dripped off Jason's chin. I think of the possibility of him kissing someone else in a snowbank, just kissing. It would bother me.

Mina tells us while we're eating that she smuggled the cheese through Customs.

She says, It's illegal outside of France, unpasteurized cheese, it's a problem with the EU. The other countries want to ban it. But the French, you can imagine how they feel. They're so passionate.

Jason lays his fork on his plate, wipes his mouth with a serviette. I put down my fork.

I say, I'm breastfeeding you know, there could be anything in that.

Mina says, We used to give our hens lobster shells and the yolks would be bright red. Bright red yolks in a cast iron skillet. Too bad this film isn't about a red insect.

She's fastening a necklace with a pendant of medicine-blue beach glass.

Fold your limbs like an insect, I say. Mina raises her arms to the back of her neck, elbows jutting. The green velvet dress she got married in.

Lean into the mirror and put on lipstick, I say.

I'm getting all this on video, then I capture stills on the computer, print them. Twenty-four pictures for one second of film. I'll loop the clip of the lipstick moving over her mouth. During the twenty-four frames her eyelids droop and close, then open. An amber ring on her finger fires a sparkle of light in frame twelve. A bar of sunlight moves over her nose and across one cheek. I'll colour the background with oil pastels, lime green, lemon, emerald, an ocean of grass.

Jason looks at the print I've tacked to the wall over the computer. He says, Mina O'Leary could be a movie star.

You think?

She has that kind of face.

Mina says, I wrote a novel while I was in France. But I used too many words. I'd rather a novel with fewer words.

Shorter, you mean?

Not necessarily shorter.

What was it about?

It was about — she looks up from her beer and adjusts the collar of her jacket, a big, distant smile as if the novel is unfolding in front of her and she likes it.

Just then a Scottish swim team crowds through the door with a blast of snowy wind. Snow on their shoulders and caps. One of them, a man with a beard full of ice and steamed glasses, interrupts Mina, begins a conversation about trade unions. The singer is doing Bruce Springsteen, snapping her fingers and tapping one foot. When she's finished she scans the audience with her hand over her eyes.

She says, I'd like my bass player to come on up, unless he's taking a leak.

She tells a filthy joke and the whole bar groans. Mina takes a notebook from her purse, writes something, tears off the page and gives it to the Scottish swimmer, who balls it up and swallows it. She laughs and lays her hand on his cheek. The team has gathered around her and they all raise their pints and give a cheer.

I say, I'm surprised anyone would tell a joke like that.

Mina's eyes narrow.

She says, I'm not surprised at all. I've seen her tend bar at the Spur, not that I go there.

All of the joy from flirting with the swim team vanishes. She is grimly considering the singer.

Finally she says, I'm not that keen on other women.

Green things. Lantern glass, John Steffler mentions. Escapes.

```
INT. ABSTRACT SPACE - DAY

Mina hammers another lobster, the crackling
of shells. She's talking to her friend. Her
face is full of the memory she's describing.

          MINA
     He took me up in his arms in the
     middle of the night. A drop fell
     from the eave onto my forehead, and
     that's how I woke. I was about
     eight, too old to be carried. He
     walked over the field of snow for a
     long time and into the woods. We
     hadn't seen him for months maybe, or
     days, I don't know. We got to a
     clearing, and there was an eclipse
     of the moon. It turned red. The moon
     was red, a bright red yolk.
```

Mina thinks Liv Ullman's face is grotesque.

She says, Her lips are so puffy, her cheeks, bone structure. Her face bugs me. But she's beautiful too. A face can be beautiful and grotesque by turns.

The thing about beauty, says her husband, it's mostly anticipation and memory.

Somehow, when she was in France, Mina met Yvonique, a
very, very rich man who was working as a bicycle courier. He
had wanted to try out work, and he'd enjoyed it, liked winding
through traffic in black spandex, lithe and rubbery as a stick of
licorice. His bike was so light he could lift it with his pinky. She
married him and brought him home. I met him for the first
time at a party. He was handing out tiny drinks called lemon
drops, which you toss over the tongue. After three of these the
black and white tiled floor karate-chopped my knees. I
demanded of Yvonique that we become blood brothers. He
took up a paring knife from the counter, wet with lemon juice
and pulp, and cut his thumb. I cut my thumb, felt the sting of
lemon, and we staggered around the crowded kitchen, yelling
and holding each other up by our joined thumbs. Mina helped
me home, through Bannerman Park, where the trees lay down
on their sides and the moon shot through the air like a high
bouncer, crazy zigzags. There was no hangover the next morning. It was as though the party hadn't happened. It made me
think their marriage couldn't last.

INT. A COMMUNITY HALL - NIGHT

The hall is crowded for a turkey-tea. A HAND-
SOME MAN in a cowboy hat sits alone on the
stage playing a guitar and singing "Your
Cheating Heart." Nobody listens.

> HANDSOME MAN
>
> Thank you very much, thank you. Now
> I'd like to invite my daughter Mina
> up here with me for a duet we've
> been practising together.

An eight-year-old Mina dressed in frilly pink
with a bow in her hair walks onto the stage
and the room goes silent.

EXT. AIRPORT RUNWAY - DAY

Eight-year-old Mina, in the frilly pink dress
and bow from before, stands on an empty runway in a blizzard. The sound of roaring
planes, descending. She looks up into the
storm trying to decide which way to run. We
hear adult Mina speak and the roar subsides.

> MINA
>
> I got a phone call while I was in
> Ottawa at a swimming competition.
> They told me there was a call. I was
> watching through a big glass window,
> girls from all over Canada, diving
> into the pool. The way they entered
> the water with hardly a splash. My
> aunt told me I had to come home, I

had to be on the next plane. I knew
he'd died somewhere, probably drunk.
That I'd never see him again.

EXT. COUNTRY ROAD - DUSK

An isolated trailer on cement blocks in the
middle of a field of dead grass and snow. One
window is lit, and we see a woman passing
back and forth. A hungry dog trots across the
lawn and disappears into the woods.

INT. BEDROOM - NIGHT

Mina is sniffing a line of coke on her vanity
table. She stares at herself in the mirror.
There is a vase of dried roses, the petals
covered with dust. She touches the petals and
a green spider drops on a thread. The bedroom
door bursts open behind her and with it the
noise of a loud party, laughter, techno
music. Her husband waves a bottle at her and
goes to the closet, grabs a tuxedo jacket, is
telling her to hurry up, but we can't hear
him over the noise. She watches him in the
mirror behind her. He shuts the door and the
room is silent. She stands and puts on a long
gold satin coat with a cream lining. She flaps

it once, twice. The fabric falls over the
lens and the screen goes gold.

We show Mina the video of my son's birth. Her face is con-
torted, her fingers gripping her toes. She writhes.

Do you want us to stop?

She puts one hand over her eyes, and drags it down her
face. For a moment I can see the pink of her under lids.

Keep going, she says.

The baby's head. I see my own fingers — reaching between
my legs trying to pull the skin of my vagina wider. The ring of
fire, a friend told me later. All the burning.

I say, It hurts, it hurts.

Jason shot video only during the contractions. During the
three minutes between contractions I was joyous. I made jokes.
The room was full of laughter. Keith Jarrett playing on the
stereo. The way he sighs, the piano bursting loudly into the
room and dragging itself out like a big wave over stones. An
ambulance attendant in training was invited to watch. He stood
in the dim part of the room in a uniform, his hands clasped
behind his back. The baby's head emerges, the doctor lifts the
cord away from the baby's shoulders. Watching the video, I am
amazed by the skill with which the doctor lifts the cord.
Unhurried, like crowning a prince, a rite that requires a lifetime
of devoted practice to perform simply.

There was a complication. The doctor's voice off camera:
We have an emergency.

Everything speeds up. The baby's head is between my legs,

the doctor's hand tugging the cord out of the way, and a giant gush of blood.

Jason puts the video on pause. On the still TV screen the splashing of blood stands out around the baby's neck like an Elizabethan collar.

That's it, says Jason, his first second in the world, right there.

He presses play and the baby's body comes out after the head and the blood flashes like a bullfighter's cape twisting in the air. I wanted to ask everyone to leave the room. I remember suddenly the desire to be alone. I wanted to die alone, and it seemed I would die. But I didn't want to offend the ambulance attendant by asking him to leave. He'd stood so straight and quiet, I can barely make him out of the dark in the video.

Everyone who reads John Steffler's poem says, Wow. Or, Pretty powerful. Everyone knows what it means to want something with such intensity you crush it in your haste to have it. I felt a terrible vertigo during those moments while the blood poured out of me. As if I were falling from a great height, and I hit the hard bed with a jolt. Jason stopped shooting then. But in the next shot on the videotape we are fine. The baby is in my arms, and I am holding the receiving blanket open, I am touching his foot.

EXT. BASILICA - NIGHT

It's midnight, New Year's Eve. People have gathered on the steps of the basilica to watch the fireworks. I'm there with my

eight-year-old and my new infant under my
coat. The fireworks fall through the night
like bright, spurting blood. Mina is standing
beside me. Horns honk, cheering, party hats.
Mina closes her eyes and the screen goes dark
for a few seconds. Silence. We see an ultra-
sound of a fetus kicking against the dark, we
see gushing champagne, then champagne bubbles
falling through the night sky, the statue of
the Virgin Mary in front of the basilica with
a mantle of snow, her hand moves just
slightly, a benediction, Mina's husband grabs
her and kisses her. The video of the birth
seen previously plays in reverse, until the
baby has disappeared, unwinding history.

I say to Mina: Now, try to look as if you are about to alight.

Craving

Jessica laughs very loud and the candle flames lie down stretched and flat. She moves the candelabra in front of her husband.

She says, I like aggressive men.

I say, I like aggressive women.

She dips her spoon into the mushroom soup.

But this is delicious, she says.

Vermouth, I say. On the way back from the liquor store a plastic bag of fierce yellow slapped against my shin. I peeled it away, meat juice coursing in the wrinkles like a living beast. It clung just as viciously to a telephone pole when I let it go. There was a poster on the pole just above the bag, Jessica Connolly at Fat Cat's. A band of men behind her. She looked resolute and charged, just like twenty years ago when the three of us would crush ourselves into a change room in the mall, forcing our bodies into the smallest-sized jeans we could find

59

EN

— she and Louise and I, twisting on the balls of our feet to see how our bums looked.

I like aggressive women too, she says.

That's because we're both aggressive.

I put my arm around Louise and squeeze her. I like you anyway, Lou, I say.

Jessica says, Oh, she's passive aggressive.

She isn't though, I say. Jessica pouts her lower lip, contemplating. We both concentrate on Louise's sweetness for a moment. Louise reaches for the bread, her brow furrowed. She's trying to think of something bad.

Lou's so wonderful, though, Jessica says, giving up. I glance at my husband. The men don't know each other. I should be drawing them into the conversation, but this is too heady. Jessica's so thoroughly herself, the genuine article.

Louise says, Do you remember when our class used to go to church? I loved the feeling of the sleeve of someone's blouse touching my arm. If they were unaware of it. Just brushing against my arm. Someone else's sleeve.

Jessica says, I love my daughter.

She's holding her spoon in the air. Jessica is far away, her eyes full of her daughter. She's in the park or the delivery room — somewhere with a lot of light — and the child is vigorous, screaming or running. Jessica sent a picture at Christmas of the four of them. The boy resting his cheek on her bare shoulder. Her daughter trying to tear off a white sunhat.

I love my son too, she says, and dips the spoon. But my daughter is going to do things. She'll get into a lot of trouble too. Jessica grins at her soup, proud and grim about the trouble her daughter's going to cause.

I tell them a story about a Bulgarian woman that ends with the shout, No matter, I must have it!

I say, This should be our motto. We clink our wine glasses and shout, No matter, I must have it! But the men go on with their conversation at the other end of the table. They are talking music, the different qualities a variety of sound systems offer.

Then Jessica says, I'm going through flux right now. Her eyes flit to her husband. I slam my hand flat on the table, the wine glasses jiggle.

Stop it, I say.

Stop what? The flux?

I won't have flux at the dinner table, I say.

Okay, she says, and she laughs, but it's more of a sly chuckle. We are twelve again, in the bloating, compressed heat of the canvas camper in her parents' driveway. She and Louise are trying to convince me I have to come out now. One of her brothers noticed my new bra and made some remark. Sitting alone in the trailer, with my arms crossed so tight over my chest that the next morning my arm muscles are stiff and it hurts to pull a sweater over my head. Jessica full of worldly disgust. Louise obstinately refusing to make Jessica relent, which she could do with a single tilt of her chin. They are united in the desire to punish my vanity. They don't have bras, but they have braces on their teeth, and that makes them a club.

Jessica says, Fine, if that's the way you want it.

I start to cry, knowing it's a gamble. Louise wavers but

Jessica's scorn fulminates into a full-blown denouncement. She won't let me ruin all the fun. It's sunny outside and the camper smells of her brother's sports socks.

They wander off, their voices fading, Jessica's ringing laugh the last sound, not a forced laugh, they have forgotten me. Then I listen to the wind through the maples, straining to hear my parents' car coming for me.

Jessica admired the characters of her Siamese cats, haughty and lascivious. She could suss out the swift-forming passions of the gang of boys we knew, and make them heel. She knew the circuit of their collective synaptic skittering and played it like pinball. She couldn't be trusted with secrets, and we couldn't keep them from her.

I ask her husband if he wants more soup. I won't play a part in excluding him, though I'm sure everything is his fault.

He says, I don't know what else is coming.

There's dessert, says Louise. Lou wants to save him from the flux too. Save us all, because it's a big wave that could make the panes in the French door explode and we'd be up to our necks with the soup bowls floating.

Then Louise's boyfriend says, But pollution is a by-product of industry and we all want industry, so. He shrugs.

Lou catches my eye. She's thinking, Remember the guy on the surfboard in Hawaii? I felt total abandon. An evanescing of self, my zest uncorked.

Yes, but if you had kept going, it wouldn't have been abandon. He wouldn't be a man swathed in the nimbus of an incandescent wave, muzzling the snarling lip of that bone-crushing maw of ocean with a flexed calf muscle. He would be one of these guys at the table, half drunk and full of mild love.

There's my husband, heavy-lidded, flushed. The first time I saw him my skin tingled with the nascent what-would-come. Shane Walker. Red suspenders tugging at his faded jeans. The best way to make a thing happen is to not want it. I didn't want him so bad that he strode right over to the table and dropped down his books, *Mexico in Crisis* and *The Marxist Revolution*. He rubs his hands down the front of his faded jeans.

I read your sexy poem, he says.

A sheet of water falling from a canoe paddle like a torn wing. That's the only line of the poem I remember. So much bald longing in a paddle stroke. A torn wing, big deal, yet Shane Walker is blushing. Then I decided — No matter, I must have it.

Jessica taps her spoon on the edge of her cup. She's furious — why won't I have flux at the dinner table? It's only emotion, everything blows over. What am I afraid of? Let Louise have her beach boy.

I think, What if it wasn't abandon? What if some part of Louise stays on a surfboard in Hawaii forever when this guy, who considers the politics of pollution, wants her. Would Jessica have Louise long eternally for something that never existed? It's perverted. And what about Jessica? How long can this last, this brave refusal to compromise? There's redemption in submission. If Jessica wants to strut her charisma I'll stand aside, but in the end she's wrong and I'm right.

Why does the end matter, shrieks Jessica, there is no end. She doesn't say anything, of course, she's gone to the bathroom.

We're only on the soup, there are several courses, whose idea was this, the plastic bag on my shin, her poster. Wouldn't it be fun? How have we changed? I think, This may be the end.

She says, I'd rather die ignited than sated.

I realize now, totally zonked — Jessica has rolled three joints since she got here, I haven't been stoned in years, it's so pleasurable, so good, I can hardly collect the plates — that I have always believed the flaws of men are born of a stupidity for which they, men, can't be held accountable. I recognize in a flash — I have balanced the sixth soup bowl, a spoon spins across the floor — that all my relations with men have been guided by this generous and condescending premise. I see now that the theory comes from the lack of courage required to face the truth, which is that men are pricks. They're aware women like me exist, women who believe they have been shafted in terms of a moral spine, and these men welcome these women's low estimation of themselves, and capitalize on it.

My neighbour, Allan, in the kitchen this afternoon while I was preparing for the dinner party. He was dropping off the flyers for the parent/teachers' auction. It disturbs me that Allan has never flirted with me. He flings himself onto a kitchen chair, spoons white sugar over a piece of bread, which he folds and eats in three bites.

He says, Aren't we all hungry?

I thought, Hungry for what? But I could remember a keening, an imminence. At certain hours it was strongest, at dawn riding my bike downhill, walking home from a bar at four in the morning.

I know I am, says Allan. I'm hungry.

I used to crave something, but what was it? Approval? It was bigger than the whole world approving, bigger than anything language could hog-tie. It compelled my every action, even eating a bran muffin I could tremble with excitement, thinking something might happen now, right now.

Allan certainly looks hungry, all shoulders and elbows splayed over the table.

I say, I can't help you, Allan.

I wasn't certain I'd spoken out loud. When I said *I can't help you*, I meant, I wish you wanted me, and even, I'd like to climb on the kitchen table with you — but I didn't say that, thankfully. What I said was terrible enough, *I can't help you*. I had been unaware, until that moment, that I wished to be desired by Allan.

He says, But I don't want you to help me.

Why wouldn't he want me too? If he is so damn hungry?

Louise: Why don't we unleash a primal battle screech, our friend is in flux for fuck's sake.

I think, Oh yes, it would be great to be Jessica. Let's all be Jessica, ready to burst into flame over an unpaid parking ticket. Ready, anyway, to sleep with the window washer who lowers himself to her office window on rope and pulley, blue overalls and cap, his powerful arms cutting slices of clarity through the soapy blur.

Fabulous, says Jessica.

We are very drunk now, it seems. Or I am, not used to

smoking, but Jessica has a bristling fixity. She flicks her wrist to look at her watch. I have to go downtown, she says.

But it's our dinner party. We haven't seen each other. We don't know how we've changed.

Her husband says, I'll come with you.

Jessica says, You have to relieve the babysitter.

I think, It's too late. I didn't do my part. I have forsaken the promises of our adolescence; hiding near the warm tires of parked cars while playing spotlight at dusk, holding still while curling irons burn our scalps, splashes of silver raining from the disco balls in the parish hall, mashed banana emollients, face scrubs with twigs and bits of apricot, ears pierced with an ice cube and sewing needle, and the disquieting loss of a belief in God. The saturated aura, a kinetic field of blue light, that surrounded a silent phone while we willed it to ring. Our periods. Dusk, all by itself, dusk, walking home from school after a volleyball game and the light withdrawing from the pavement. I look at my husband, I try to feel dissatisfied but I can't, he's a beautiful man.

Jessica's husband wants her to give him money for the babysitter but she won't. She's angry he didn't take care of it himself. The chink of a wine glass on the marble fireplace. Louise's boyfriend rises from his chair and sways a little, he moves across the room and pats Jessica on the head.

Patronizing bitch, he says.

Jessica grins. She unfurls a peel of giggles tinny as a dropped roll of tinfoil bouncing across the kitchen tiles. She picks up her leather jacket and fires up the zipper. She grabs me by the shoulders, presses me into her big breasts. Then she holds me at arm's length.

You, she says, haven't changed a bit.

She moves to Louise, lifts her from the couch also by the shoulders, gives her a big hug.

She kisses her husband on both cheeks and hands him forty bucks.

She says, I love you, even at this moment.

She says to Louise's boyfriend, You, I'm not hugging.

She opens the French door and the window panes rattle.

Thank you so much, it was lovely.

The front door slams behind her. We each sit up a little, adjusting our posture, the draft from the front door sobering. Outside the dining-room window, we can hear her platform heels slapping the sidewalk, she has broken into a trot.

Natural Parents

Lyle and Anna hardly speak on the way to the Ivanys' dinner party. At a red light on Empire, Anna asks him what he thinks the Ivanys will serve. Lyle says he doesn't know.

They drive past the graveyard. There's a group gathered in the dark, huddled near a canopy covering an open and empty grave. A woman on the edge of the group holds a fat bunch of yellow roses wrapped in plastic, the blossoms hanging down toward the mud. Anna can't think what they're doing in the graveyard at night. The roses are vibrant against the woman's black coat. They look like they're floating. An angel grave marker near the chainlink fence of the graveyard has snow on her wings and in her eye sockets, on her bottom lip. The chain-link is furred over with snow too. The woman with the roses speaks to the man beside her. He tilts an ear toward her.

Lyle pumps the brakes and the car slides sideways, the rear swinging like a boat pushed away from the dock. A Cadillac, grey and graceful as a dolphin, plows nose first through a deep, curving drift on the opposite sidewalk. Anna throws her arm over and back, grabbing for Pete's car seat. Lyle stops just before they nudge the bumper in front of them. The light changes; they pass the graveyard.

Anna says, I know what I wish they were serving. I'd like a roast, a nice bloody hunk of meat.

Lyle says, That's probably what it'll be.

No, it won't, she says. She feels so tired that she just wants to go home. She's angry with Lyle because he's enthusiastic about the party. He's a herd of wild horses, he's already abandoned her. Thrumming the wheel with his leather-covered fingers. They haven't discussed who will stay sober, but it was decided long ago, perhaps when she discovered she was pregnant. He gets to drink; she doesn't. He rolls down the window and wipes the windshield with an old newspaper. Cold wind and snow blow through the car.

Some night, he says.

She flips open the makeup mirror in the sun visor to check on Pete. He's asleep, the snowsuit hood cupping his face, his tiny eyebrows bent with concentration.

He hasn't been sleeping much lately. It's an ear infection, or cutting teeth, Anna doesn't know why. Wait it out, the doctor said. But she and Lyle have aged more in the last three weeks than they have in the last twelve years. Last night, at two-thirty, Pete started to cry and Lyle threw off the blankets and just sat on the edge of the bed, his elbows resting on his knees, his hands covering his face. Anna waited for Lyle to move but he didn't.

I wanted to be doing other things at this stage in my life, he said.

What other things?

Sleeping, for one.

Anna felt for her glasses and put them on. Pete was standing in the crib, gripping the bars. Anna switched on the bedside lamp and she could see the lines of his tears shining in the bar of lamplight. Pete drew a deep breath, his body became rigid. He inhaled and there was absolutely no sound. His mouth wide open, his face getting redder and redder. Anna imagined the whole universe being sucked into his tiny body, she and Lyle, their eleven-year-old daughter, Alex, the telephone poles, grimy snowbanks, loose pennies, Christmas presents, the Atlantic, asteroids. Then it reversed. Pete tilted his head back and the world, ragged and inconsolable, came back out. She heard, from just below the bedroom window, a snowplow lowering its shovel, the arthritic grinding and ringing clang as the grizzled teeth of the plow hit the pavement, then the wheeze of brakes before the warning bell. The white blinds of their bedroom turning apocalyptic blue and underworld orange by turns. She hadn't expected to feel old.

Anna said, Are you going to do something here, Lyle?

Lyle didn't answer, so Anna got up and took Pete out of the cot. She switched on the overhead light.

What do you want me to do, Lyle asked. His hands had dropped from his face so they hung over his knees, but he didn't lift his head. He was looking at the floor. She told him to go back to sleep.

But what about you? He sounded genuinely baffled. He had never wanted children, any children, but once they came he tried to do his share. He found Pete's bottle in the blankets of the crib and went down the hall, stopping at his daughter's bedroom.

Alex was sleeping with her arm thrown over the dog, whose back legs were hanging open, his penis distended and raw looking, the balls shiny with short, silvery hair, pink skin showing beneath. They needed to get the dog neutered; he was barking in the garden, even with the muzzle, and the neighbours were complaining. A crayon had melted onto the radiator and the room smelled of burning dust and wax, fusty and fruity, like cherries and velvet. The quilt had slid off Alex's bed. Her pyjamas were printed with red umbrellas, the dye was bleeding so each gale-tossed umbrella had a pink aura. The window opaque with frost, Alex's mouth parted — her bottom lip gleaming in the sepia light from downtown — all of this woke Lyle up. He was awake. Finally, irrevocably alert.

Lyle pulled the blanket up to Alex's chin. He stood there remembering a summer afternoon last year when he and Alex had gone swimming at Archibald Falls, near the house they had in Conception Bay. The falls were a long hike into the woods, and he and Alex were usually the only ones there. They'd picked wild strawberries and blackberries, eating them as they went. Then they'd put on yellow-tinted goggles and watched two small trout swimming in circles just below the waterfall's ramrod, feathery spine. Afterwards they sat on the lichen-splattered boulders and read their books together.

Standing at the foot of Alex's bed with the empty baby bottle in his hand, Lyle felt that specific summer afternoon roaring through him. The thrashing of the falls, the smell of wild roses, and when the wind shifted, a sweet, poisonous smoke from a dump far off in the hills. In the evening he had heated beans and made scrambled eggs on the Coleman stove for supper. They ate outside, reading as they ate. It had been a full day of reading. They'd hardly spoken but had achieved an unequivocal harmony until the boy from next door had waded through the grass. The boy was Alex's age, just eleven, with a jagged haircut and freckles, his eyes pale blue and commanding. He held before him, on a Dominion bag, a fresh cod. Without a word, Alex had turned her book over so the library plastic crackled. She hooked her dangling sneaker over her heel with one finger and followed the boy around the corner of the house.

Lyle watched them through the wavering old glass of the kitchen window while he washed the dishes. The kitchen smelled of wood smoke and bitter crabapples. Lyle's dog, Sic'um, tore through the grass after the boy until the nylon rope snapped taut and drops of water and mist were flung from it to hang iridescent over the grass and the dog boomeranged a couple of feet back. The children stood still, facing each other. The boy joined his hands in front of his chest and bowed deeply. Then he clenched his fists near his hips, lifted his foot high above his shoulder and swung it with slo-mo gentleness toward Alex's chin. She pretended the foot had caught her jaw. She began a flailing, ballerina dive into the grass, where she disappeared. The boy stood waiting as though he were watching a lake for a swimmer who had been under too long. Then he dove into the long grass where Alex had disappeared. They stayed there, in the grass. When Alex came inside to help with dishes she was overtaken by a self-absorption Lyle had never seen in her before. When she finally met his eyes — he had lit the kerosene lamp and the darkness of the kitchen had cupped them like two giant palms cupping a moth — she seemed surprised to see him. She'd said, Girls in my class wear training bras. She was mangling a slice of bread with a knife and gob of butter. Of course, she'd said, I don't have anything to *put* in a bra. She looked up and her whole face was rosy with shame and exultation.

After they'd cleaned up they went outside, where there was still enough light to read. Their books were damp, a fine, settling dew put a wave in the pages of his Heidegger. They read together until the boy returned, beating the grass with a plastic hockey stick. He wanted Alex to play spotlight.

Lyle looked up from his book. Reading Heidegger that afternoon, Lyle had been like someone copying pans of ice, desperate to cover distance, grasping a difficult phrase only long enough to leap to the next. A fast squall of grace had raced across the ice to engulf him. He had dipped a gingersnap into his coffee while he read, and had forgotten it was there in his hand.

But there was the boy and his daughter, the fringe of her cut-offs, red flashing lights in the soles of her sneakers. The cookie had sopped up so much coffee that it was falling over, and he caught it in his mouth. Alex's face: the big, new teeth, her sunburned, peeling nose, her fiercely blue eyes, a moist film of perspiration near her temple. He felt a physical ache in his chest because she was so unspeakably beautiful to him. Then he couldn't remember what he had been reading, the argument fell apart. When he glanced back at the book the letters were fuzzy. It was too dark to continue reading. This was why he hadn't wanted kids. They were a constant interruption. The field of loose ice sank away, nothing remaining but a phrase, *the abandonment of being*, which might have been Sanskrit. Where had Anna been that day? She was pregnant with Pete. Lyle had watched the pale arm of the flashlight riffling through the trees.

Anna said, Lyle, are you getting the bottle? Because I'm waiting here.

He was a man dreaming he was a butterfly dreaming he was a man. The winter night asserted itself. Snow pinging the glass. He could hear music, from downtown. The red *S* of the Scotiabank was in the top right corner of Alex's window, it had a chef's hat of snow glowing pinkly.

When Lyle was eighteen he'd slept with a girl named Rachel he'd met in first year university. Rachel was seventeen and he slept with her maybe half a dozen times. The first time, they'd met in the Breezeway, a raucous university bar with roving coloured spotlights.

They had never made an effort to get together after that; they'd just happen upon each other. The last time they met like this was in the wind tunnel between the library and the chemistry building. She was wearing a long candy-cane striped

scarf. It stood out in front of her, rippling. The wind was blowing her across a skim of ice and she was squealing and she slid
into his arms. Their chests smacked, and when he bent his
nose into the icy fox-fur trim he could smell her lipgloss.

It was four-thirty in the afternoon, already dark. His wrists
stuck out of the leather gloves his mother had insisted he wear
and he remembered that his wristbones felt like glass, that a
sharp bang might have cleanly snapped off his hands. It was
below zero. They'd gotten a bus to her parents' house. The windows of the bus were grey with salt and a man sat beside him
with crutches that cuffed his forearms and his legs were twisted
and stiff like pipe cleaners.

Rachel told Lyle he should stop reading philosophy. She
said, Literature is such a kick. You've got to read that. And she
looked out the window over her shoulder as if one of the stout,
soft-covered Penguins she had jammed in her knapsack —
Middlemarch, Anna Karenina, or *Crime and Punishment* — was
unfolding on the street. He told her his wrists were cold and
she took the glove off his right hand and put her searing mouth
over his wristbone so it bristled with needles like a startled
porcupine.

When they arrived at her parents' house, somewhere in
Mount Pearl, she lifted a curled real estate guide from the mail-
box, a hardened baton sheathed in ice. She poked his stomach
with it, and when he looked down she slapped his cheek. The
ice on the guide smashed to pieces that skittered across the
concrete step. The slap left a sting.

That was for nothing, she said, don't try anything. She

turned her back on him and unlocked the door and he followed her inside.

They smoked some pot in the bathroom, a white gauzy curtain gone yellow with age flying out the open window against the night sky. That evening of lovemaking has come over him lots of times since; often when he's tired or drunk, it overtakes him, haunts him, so he can almost smell the crackling hope of the new subdivision, the whiff of cedar and camphor in the pink bedspread ruffles that had been unexpectedly rough against his cheek, the stinky dope meeting the stormy wind. There had been a marmalade cat with a fluffy tail drawing up the gold and rust shag carpet with her nails, very near his ear, on the living-room floor.

Pot exacted from him a languid thoroughness while making love. Every touch lost its path, outlived its life expectancy. She had licked under his arm, and that cool trail he'd felt for days afterward, while washing dishes for his mother, dopey with the steam rising from the sink and the heat of the oven, or while lazing on the living-room carpet before *Gilligan's Island* and *Get Smart* with the slippery velvet of the golden retriever's ear in his fingers. The cheeks of her bum, breasts like saucers of snowflakes, smoky breath, the bitten-down fingernails with chipped blue polish. He'd held her arms over her head, both of her wrists in one hand. He'd lowered her bra with his teeth, uncovering a nipple so it peeked out from a crush of eyelet lace, and he could feel with his tongue the roughness of the cotton and the softness of just the very tip of the pink, pink nipple. When his tongue touched her there she squirmed against him. What a shock her mouth was. A hot, working muscle, a current, a force.

After they had taken off each other's clothes she went into the kitchen for a drink of water. They had a fridge with a door that made crushed ice, and it was the first time he'd seen one. It was super-modern, a reflective black that matched the other appliances. She held the glass under a spout in the door of the fridge and the machine growled and the glass filled with slush. She drank the whole glass and filled it again, stopping to grin at him, wiping a drip from her chin with the back of her hand. She was wearing a fat mood ring, and it was dark green, which meant, she said, that she was fuckable. He lifted her, taking a cheek of her bum in each of his hands, surprised by how light she was. Her legs wrapped over his hips and her back was pressed against the door of the fridge. With each thump they heard jars rattling, glass clinking; something smashed, the engine whirred, her hand slapped the black door three times. A Reddi-Kilowatt magnet scuttled along the gleaming surface to the floor.

Rachel spilled the ice over his chest, it felt like flankers spat from a fire and a line of it glittered in their joined bellies, it dug into his thighs. It crunched in their pubic hair, and when he came it felt like his veins were running with blue antifreeze, so cold it made sweat spring to his forehead. He kissed her mussy hair. Her bum squeaked against the black door as he set her on her feet. Her mouth was cold from the water, like an igloo.

She switched on a fluorescent light and they both began to giggle. The copper cooking pots hung over the stove in order of diminishing size, there was an Esso calendar with a picture of a terrier, a red and white gingham apron tossed over the back of a pine chair, a box of Ritz crackers. Their nakedness boinged forward like something on a trampoline. Nothing in the room had been altered by their sex. The kitchen immured their glittering, star-struck bodies in a sheath of bland fluorescence without giving them a thought.

The marmalade cat eyed Lyle through the kitchen doorway. She came into the room and raised her tail. She rubbed herself against the fridge, jutted her chin, and then crossed the black and white tiles to weld her static coat to Lyle's bare calf. The street had turned a perfect, uncanny white. An errant draft raised goosebumps on Lyle's arms. A rectitude stole over him with the chill. There was a sinister note in the freedom he felt in her parents' kitchen. Rachel had been digging in the cupboard and had taken out a tin of chocolate chip cookies. She piled them on the counter and fit the lid back on the illustrated tin; it was the Norman Rockwell of a little girl with a pink bow in her hair and her drawers lowered for a spanking, ink hand prints on the wall behind her.

Ravenous, Rachel said, her mouth filled with cookie.

A paranoia shot through him, made his heart take off the way a cartoon heart, the Road Runner's, might stretch through his brown fur and hang in the air while the rest of his spindly body fell miles and miles to the dusty earth. Lyle couldn't get his jeans on fast enough, hobbling down the hallway from Rachel's bedroom with one pant leg flapping to the side, nearly falling as he dragged the waist over his knees, leaving behind him a trail of coins.

He had not walked very far down the new cul-de-sac when a car passed him, plastering a sheet of slush to his shins. The car pulled into Rachel's driveway. Her parents sat for a moment, and then they got out. They had groceries. He watched them make their way up the path. Her mother's long coat was a gash of fuchsia. He was close enough to hear the aluminum storm door smack behind them. The living-room light came on. He stayed, he had no idea how long, but nothing else happened. The house remained inert. He stood under the streetlight and watched the snowflakes.

He was overwhelmed with the joy of not being caught. He made a decision, almost a pledge, that he would not sleep with Rachel again. He probably wouldn't even run into her, but if he did he wouldn't speak much to her. Lovers slipped out of his life when he was eighteen without consequence. He decided the freedom he'd felt in her kitchen would just be the start. He made a resolution: beam a mild vertigo from your forehead at all times, like a miner's lamp. In this way you'd always step to the side when ruin tore down the path behind you. You'd always get out before the parents came home. He knew he was stoned but he could never discern which perception, stoned or straight, was most accurate. He promised himself he'd keep one set of thoughts in his left hand and the other set in his right.

When the phone rang several weeks later Lyle knew by the sound of his mother's voice it was a girl. His mother said that any girl who called a boy's house had no self-respect. She spoke loud enough to be overheard. The receiver was lying on a long roll of cotton batting with opalescent sparkles and tiny white

Christmas lights buried beneath it. Ceramic angels with velvet costumes and paper songbooks were stationed all over the cotton batting. Among them, the receiver looked like an alien spacecraft.

Rachel just said his name, Lyle.

It made Lyle think of when he first got contact lenses. He had stepped out of the optometrist's office on LeMarchant Road and looked up into the branches of a tree and saw, for the first time, individual leaves. Each leaf distinct from the next, rather than the loose weave of luminous, swimming colour he had always believed a tree to be. His own subjectivity, previously transparent, became opaque. He saw his mother's dark tweed sleeve shot through with minute white seeds, shiny where worn, bristling microscopic hairs of wool. He'd just had time to grasp the sleeve in his fist before he hit the sidewalk. He had fainted.

Hearing Rachel say his name while standing in his own living room. The music of *Jeopardy*, a screech from the oven hinges as his mother took out the shepherd's pie. The garburator eating a vibrant clot of carrot peelings — all of this was so altered by Rachel's voice that he almost fainted for the second time in his life.

She said she wanted to talk to him *in person*. Who had put her up to this? He guessed the counsellor at school, a young feminist with burgeoning, aggressive-looking plants in her window and a box of wooden penises she dragged around the classrooms to show how a condom works. He couldn't think how Rachel had gotten his number.

The city sifted through the fist of a snowstorm. Ribbed icicles dripped and shot sparkles. The snow was pink or buttery, blue in the scoops and caves. Shimmery veils flew in twisting sheets off the roofs and the lips of drifts. He knew what the call was about but tried to convince himself otherwise the whole way to the university. Perhaps she thought she could move the relationship to a different plane. As if a relationship were something you took into your own hands. He knew what was coming was big. And if this woman wanted to exert her will over him, such a thing might qualify as big. Maybe she was in love with him. Love might be enough to explain the portentous anxiety he felt.

Lyle had been sleeping with girls since he was thirteen. He'd been an altar boy early Sunday mornings, carrying smoking incense in an ornate silver and blood-dark glass container that hung from chains and banged against his red and white polyester robes as he walked, listening to guitar and folk hymns, and though he'd intuited the cloying menace, the oily funk of lust from a few older, eccentric men who somehow hung around the same places he did — behind the new Kmart on Topsail Road, the rectory, the pool at St. Augustine's — he had managed to avoid overt unpleasantness. He'd developed a guiltless and generous sexuality.

For instance: he'd had sex in a mouldy rec room that had a black, vinyl-padded bachelor bar ordered from the Sears catalogue and a plaid couch with dangerous springs, while pressing a glass painted with hearts, diamonds, spades, and clubs, grey with dope smoke, to his mouth, sucking it so the rim left a white circle on his face when he pried the glass away. The girl had drawn a heart with his name in ballpoint pen beneath her white school blouse. Sex in a friend's bedroom with a black light and black velvet KISS posters. The girl had green, greasy eyeliner and a bottle of Blue Nun, Donovan sang about the season of the witch, and his friends played Dungeons and Dragons in the next room. Sex in a pickup near a field full of fog and horses. He and the girl were washed in a bath of red light, and before he knew what was happening a cop rapped on the steamed-over window. When Lyle lowered it, the cop stuck a flashlight in and swivelled it around, catching the girl's breast, her naked foot. In the field beside them, a white horse had tossed its head, snorted, and trotted away into the fog. Once he'd taken some acid with a friend and two sixteen-year-old twin girls in a prefab cabin just beyond the overpass. He and his friend were sitting on one bed and the girls were sitting opposite them, a case of beer at their feet, when the twins' father crashed through the door with a rifle. The door hit the wall and the cabin shuddered, a watercolour of a moose in Bowring Park swung back and forth from the jolt. The moose's jaw fell, and moss and water poured into the lake at his knees, gently rippling the surface. The pink wallpaper expanded like bubblegum, stretching until it was a concave membrane, semi-transparent. Lyle hallucinated the trees behind the wall and the path to the mini-golf castle and duck pond, and he was confident he could simply step through to the other side if the screaming father took aim.

So, up to this point, he'd had lots of sex but he knew

nothing about girls. Everything about them — the elaborate knowledge they had of each other's emotional states, how whole oceans of thought could be traversed in a gesture, the sophisticated designs of cruelty they visited upon each other without prompting — he didn't understand any of it. This ignorance gave him courage now, walking in the storm toward the university.

By the time he got to the campus it was deserted. Lyle thought Rachel probably wouldn't show up. He promised himself that if he escaped this time he'd never take another chance, feeling in one moment that he meant it, promising God, his mother. Knowing in the next moment, watching his body wobble like the flame of a candle reflected in the chemistry building windows, that if he did escape, it was a promise he'd forget instantly.

Rachel was the only person in the cafeteria, except a janitor at the far end of the room putting the orange chairs upside down on the tables. The fluorescent lights thrummed. She was wearing a black T-shirt with a marijuana leaf on the front. There was a bran muffin in front of her on a Styrofoam plate. A plastic glass of juice with the foil lid folded back. She was wearing dark sunglasses, and when he saw them he knew she wasn't in love.

He dragged out the chair beside her and the metal legs screeched like a bird caught in an engine. Before he sat down she said she was pregnant and she wouldn't consider abortion. He said, Are you sure? By which he meant, Are you sure I'm the father. She knew what he meant and she was hurt by the question, and that surprised him more than anything. Their sexual encounters had a different meaning for her. Perhaps every sexual encounter he'd ever had had meant something different to the girl. She had summoned him through a blizzard. He had implicated himself by showing up. He was there.

The child, a little girl, was three by the time Lyle met Anna. She stayed with Lyle for half the week until she was seven, and then he and Rachel agreed it was easier for everyone if she lived in one place. He paid child support, and drove her to hockey and ballet. She came for supper when she felt like it.

One day last March I went up to Lyle's study on the third floor. I pushed Sic'um out of the armchair near the window. It had occurred to me that we might, after twelve years together, split up over this. I wondered what would happen to our house, the summer house in Conception Bay, the car. How would Alex feel. I was still wearing my winter coat. I held the bag from the pharmacy.

This is it, I said. I rattled the bag. Lyle swivelled in his chair to face me. He pressed his hands down the length of his thighs. I had wanted a second child more than anything in the world and Lyle hadn't. I had wanted one with all my might. Alex was eleven.

Go to it, he had said. While I was in the bathroom reading the instructions I could hear him typing.

We had been vacationing in France. I was in the shower and I'd felt a sharp pinch and knew. It was like anything else without rhythm or beat. No way to be sure of it; I was sure. My forehead tingled, I broke a light sweat. All the objects in the world brightened in a single synchronic pulse. If Lyle wanted to leave, he could leave. If there was a fight, I would hardly be able to pay attention. Nobody feels conception taking place; I felt it.

The wheels on Lyle's office chair squeaked over my head. The test sat on the windowsill. The bathroom linoleum was cold underfoot and there was a flattened squiggle of blue toothpaste in the sink with some of Alex's hair stuck in it, wavering under a thread of water from the leaking tap. On the floor above, Lyle was rolling toward the bookshelf. Dragging himself with the heels of his shoes. Then he kicked himself back to the computer and began typing again. Our luggage was still in the living room, though we'd been back a week. I wanted it put away. Beside the pregnancy test, an enamel soap dish, a brilliant white bar of soap smeared with two bleating red petals from the geranium. The faded pink cross on the plastic wand turned redder.

I called up the stairs, It's positive.

Lyle rings the doorbell and we wait. Prissy Ivany swings the door wide open and grins at us. She's wearing a long, clingy black dress with a greenish sheen and her hair is big and orange.

Your hair is beautiful, Prissy, I say. Charles Ivany comes up behind his wife.

She once hid some forks in there, Charles says.

That's true, says Prissy, a whole place setting.

Where's Alex, asks Charles.

A sleepover, I say.

Charles is smoking with an emerald cigarette holder and he's wearing a tuxedo jacket with satin lapels and a red bow tie. He has a miniature set of antlers on his bald head.

So glad you could make it, he says. Let me take your coats.

Let's get that baby settled away, says Prissy. Charles claps his hands once.

What will you have to drink? I've got a very good sherry.

I'll try the sherry, Lyle says. He's beaming happiness.

Good man, says Charles.

Prissy brings me to a bedroom upstairs and helps me with the folding playpen. She switches on a baby monitor and holds it to her ear. Then she gives it a shake.

Guess that thing works, she says. When we come back downstairs Charles is telling a story about Thomas Aquinas.

Just stopped writing. Charles pauses to grin at everyone.

He'd had a vision. Everything he'd written before was straw. Charles throws back his head and laughs.

Can you imagine, *straw*, it was all straw.

Blue diodes are the next thing, Joanne Barker announces. That's all you'll hear from now on, blue diodes.

What about pocket calculators, Lyle says, didn't some calculator guy get the Nobel?

Don't start with me, says Joanne. She raises her chin at Lyle, saucy and flirting.

I want to do what Diane McCarthy always does, says Prissy. Each man moves two chairs down before dessert. Men, desert your wives.

Listen, says Lyle. Everyone hushes at once. Pete has started to cry.

I walk out to the car, Pete in one arm, the folded playpen banging against my shin. I throw it into the trunk, strap Pete into the car seat. There's a J. J. Cale tape in the stereo and it bursts honeyed and sweltering into the frosty air. *Magnolia, you sweet thing, you're driving me mad.* Fat snowflakes drift onto the windshield. The steering wheel is too cold to hold. Somewhere in the world there are magnolias. There are men who love women, a particular woman, to the point of devotion. In that part of the world babies sleep under filmy mosquito nets while their parents drink iced tea or have sex in the hammock. The babies sleep because they are overcome with muggy, perfumed heat, or maybe there are no babies. I wonder if I am too drunk to drive. I wonder it even as I sail through a red light on Elizabeth Avenue. The man in a grey fedora whose car I nearly cream has a face of pinched putty. His mouth hangs open. Pete is wide awake, he's watching the snow. When we were driving through an industrial park last week Alex had said, What if we're all dead and we only think we're alive?

This is what happened in France. This is how I got pregnant after eleven years of wanting nothing so much as to feel a child moving in my belly again. A medieval village with lace curtains in the windows and swirling cobbled streets, a castle built in a mountain pass. Isobel lost the car keys at the beach and took everything out of her knapsack, crusty socks, Don DeLillo, shaking away the sand. A goat with a chawed blue rope tied to its neck leaped onto my chest, left cloven mud prints on my blouse. An elderly woman invited us into her home, gave us port. There were four weasels glued to tree stumps on her high shelves. They killed my rabbits, she said. We saw the Papal Palace. Far below the palace grounds there is a prison, the courtyard formed by the walls draped with a fine green netting. Once a prisoner escaped in a helicopter. A girl stood on the wall and screamed to her boyfriend in a dark prison window. Did you get my message? A tattoo of a skull peeked over the drawstring waist of her pants. A field that flashed emerald, lime, yellow, and blue as the clouds drifted. A double rainbow. A sky like cashmere shredded on the blades of the mountains. A pig farm with the wind blowing toward us. Run by only one man and several computers, Lucien said. Lucien on a zigzagging unicycle, the whites of his eyes showing under the iris as he watched the silver bowling pins he juggled. Sugar cubes wrapped in a paper that says Daddy. In Marseilles a haughty waiter rolled his eyes. Alex bought sunglasses with lenses like houseflies from a black man with cornrows who jiggled his leg madly and stared in the other direction while she tried every pair. We slept on a sailboat docked in the harbour, forest of white masts pricking the indigo sky. A woman in a far-off window looked over a square, a child sleeping against her shoulder. Lamb kabobs roared on a grill, hissing and spitting fat. We picked almonds off the ground. I had my thirty-seventh birthday. Lyle slapped the cake down and the plate spun in tight, tiny circles and I shouted, Why do you always get what you want?

Bernard grew up in Paris sitting around the gypsy campfires, he tells us while he slices tomato. He is a friend of Lucien and Isobel, with whom we are staying.

I'm trying to find my parents, he says, on the computer. They have a program. He lays the tomato slices on a platter, layering them like limp dominoes.

Somewhere in Algeria, he says. I have a name.

His gut hangs over his belt and his teeth are yellow, some are missing. Sacks under his eyes. He's short compared to Lyle, his skin is swarthy. He sticks a red pepper with the point of the knife and brings it to the stove. He lights the propane and lays the pepper on the blue flame. He takes a round of fresh mozzarella out of his knapsack and slices it. He turns the pepper and the skin is blackened and blistered. He argues about Picasso. Everything in French and I can't follow, but he turns to me, pointing the tip of the knife.

Picasso's not for the common people, he says. The vehemence is thrilling. I like that he doesn't know who his parents are. I make my decision.

What's he saying about Picasso, I ask Isobel.

Bernard is a bullshit artist, she whispers.

Bernard stays the night because of the rainstorm. He's afraid of lightning. He tells me that if I am on a mountain road it's possible the lightning will pour down the hill like water and pool at my feet. If this happens I should crouch on the nearest boulder. Be careful not to dip my toe, no matter how beautiful it looks. The electricity goes out and we all gather at the window to watch the lightning over the mountains. The thunder rolls and cracks. We can hear the cows lowing, we can hear their bells. Someone is whacking them with a switch. I think: Part of the world lives with stinky, delicious cheese and weasels with glass eyes. Part of the world hates Picasso. Part of the world dances around a bonfire.

We are eating ice cream from the carton. Alex is asleep with a white sheet wrapped tight around her in the next room. The lightning zaps the snaggled interlocking branches of the olive grove. Lightning flushes through the grove like blue blood pulsing in organic tissue.

It's getting closer, I say to Bernard, whose breath I can feel on the back of my neck. I regret saying it because in the next minute I understand from the particular heat or smell coming from him, or the quality of his breathing, his stillness, that Bernard is terrified. We are all huddled in the window. He's a chef during the winter season. I didn't decide. At no point did I make a decision.

Lyle and his sister Isobel and her boyfriend Lucien run into the garden to gather the laundry. It's already so heavy with rain the sheets are dragging in the mud. We watch them dash back and forth in the battering lightning. It is monstrous and ancient, insubstantial, lethal, full of bliss. Something that might pick them up in its long pointy fingernails and fling them across the field. Bernard is rubbing circles on the cheeks of my ass with the flat of his hands while I lean against the windowsill watching them below. The lightning is stomping toward us on rickety legs; one gnarled, X-rayed bone pierces the mud, then the other. It keeps coming. Lyle and Isobel and Lucien are running under the wet sheets, they are like trapped moths beating their wings inside an overturned glass. Bernard presses a knee between my legs and spreads them apart. He crunches up my cotton skirt in his hands. He slides my underwear down to my knees. I am leaning on the window, the stone sill digging into my elbows. When he comes I think, unbidden, of something that I've heard about tuna. That if they die while panicking you can taste the fear in their flesh.

This thing with Bernard only took a minute. I swear that when the lights came back on and everybody burst back in soaked and loaded down with wet, muddy sheets Bernard and I did not exchange one complicit glance. It wasn't sweet, nor was it scurrilous. Pete looks like Lyle. Or his expressions, his smile, look like Lyle's.

It's past four in the morning and Lyle hasn't come back from the Ivanys'. I want him to come home. My arms ache from walking Pete. I sit in the cold living room, Pete wrapped in a quilt, and watch David Letterman. He shows a video clip of himself chasing a man in a chicken suit. He grabs a fire extinguisher and sprays the man, who lifts his knees high and grabs at his tail feathers as if this is hurting. A taxi pulls up outside and I turn off the TV and stand in the dark behind the lace curtain to watch for Lyle. But a giant blob of silver helium balloons bobs out of the cab, and a woman's boot tests the slush. It's my next-door neighbour. Her boyfriend comes around to her door and holds her by the elbow. He stands beside her while she struggles with her keys. He is looking into the sky, his breath frosty. He turns her from the door and takes the collar of her jacket in his hands and draws her to him and kisses her for a long time. Then she tries the keys again and the door opens and they go inside and pull the balloons in behind them.

Pete starts to cry. His body straightens, goes stiff, he almost squirms out of my arms. His cheeks are flushed. He tangles some of my hair in his fist and pulls it out. I lift it away from his hand. I get out his snowsuit and lay it on the carpet and push his arms and legs into it. I go out to the car and put Pete in the car seat and start it and wait for it to warm up. I want to drive past the Ivanys'. See Lyle's silhouette against the living-room curtains.

But I decide instead to go to the Fountain Spray. I try to think if we are out of anything, and we are. We're out of milk. But I am stopping because it's open. Because of the fluorescent orange signs that say Sale. The longer I stay away from home the more likely Lyle will be there when I get back. I'll know as soon as I look at the front of the house if he's inside, though it may not be altered in any physical way. Or it will be altered in a way I don't register consciously. Footprints in the snow. I stop for the name, too, the Fountain Spray. I will say later, So at four in the morning there I was at the Fountain Spray buying milk. Some comic telling of the life without sleep. Though it hasn't had that name for years. Needs, it's called now. Needs. There's a young man leaning over the counter with the paper. His arms crossed, he's rocking as he reads. The radio slightly off the station. Celine Dion, the song from *Titanic*. There's a stand with a giant pyramid of lemons. Even in the garish light of the all-night convenience store the lemons are blaring with colour.

I think of the woman with the yellow roses in the graveyard and wonder if I dreamed her. It's been so long since I've slept. The waking world creeps into the dreaming one. The young man, a boy really, looks up and closes the paper. The man who crashes the door against its frame shattering the glass and who then draws a hunting knife out of his filthy khaki jacket isn't as incongruous as the lemons. I've seen him in the streets lots of times muttering vengefully. I have crossed the street to avoid him. I've seen him waiting in the early morning hours for Theatre Pharmacy to open so he can get a prescription. In a few seconds he has wrenched most of the boy's body out over the counter, cut a slice through the boy's pale blue shirt. The shirt sleeve is muddied fast and sticks to the boy's arm, it darkens quickly, down to the cuff. The rack with bars and gum stands in my way. Pete starts to cry. The man turns to look at us. I can see his fist on the boy's shirt, twisting it. Perhaps the boy can't breathe. A big jar of pickled eggs falls off the counter and the fat, limbless eggs trundle across the floor as if they have places to see. A stand of chips falls over with hardly a sound. A truism: There are always innocent bystanders. I understand myself to be a bystander.

Pete and I, like extras in a movie. It's the over-brightness, the late hour, I check myself over the way a continuity girl would size up an extra, to see if my presence is necessary, believable. My suede coat with a fur collar, the belt hanging loose from the belt loops, the Velcro flap on my boot sticking out. They are tired boots with wavy lines of salt. My feet are wet. The Velcro gives when I walk and I have to bend over, with Pete in my arms, in the mall or near the parking meter outside the supermarket, to secure the flap, and it gives again. The boots are baffed out. An expression my mother-in-law uses. The essence of Lyle's mother flits through my head. She is part of the gushing collide of loves and hates and non-moments of my life that is just now thrown into sharp relief. Pete's forest green snowsuit. My fawn gloves, misshapen, a hole in the thumb. I am flabbergasted to find that the evening is bottomless. The continuity girl tallies the accumulating texture, the nuance of each detail I bring to the scene. I appear to be exactly what I am. A woman with a toddler in a convenience store during a hold-up. I am an obdurate subplot, stubbornly present. How did I get here?

But every bystander at four in the morning is brought to a convenience store by some aberration in their regular schedule. A disruption no more or less dramatic than the one that has brought me here. I am here because I believe in retribution, have been half waiting for it, half longing for the relief it might bring, ever since the night with Bernard. This is a come-uppance, an answering for, a just reward. That is my motivation as an extra in this scene, if extras need motivation. The man with the knife turns to me. If he was brought here by supernatural voices, they are telling him now, *Not the boy, dummy, the woman.* I'm not an innocent bystander. Sirens so far away they could be out in the Atlantic. Policemen. Someone shouts, Don't move. But I am at the door, and then a punch in the guts by a force so powerful it knocks the breath out of my lungs. I am drilled open by a pillar of granite. I am knocked off my feet and

I'm driven across the tiles until my head smacks the beer cooler at the far end of the store. Cans and boxes, everything flies in my face. I'm drowning.

The baby was ripped from my arms though my every thought was to keep him there. My arms are crossed over my chest as though he's still in them. But he isn't. I am holding only myself. A firehose. I am in four inches of water. Everywhere there are bobbing lemons. There are more lemons than anything else. Pete is floating face up in his snowsuit. I lurch toward him, grip the front of his suit in my fist. The water gives him up with a smack like a kiss. We are both screeching with our mouths wide and our faces red.

The doctor at Emergency checks Pete's bones, his heart, blood pressure. He looks in Pete's ears. Pete is perfectly fine; the snowsuit is waterproof; he's not even wet. I phone the Ivanys and get the machine. They've gone downtown.

I am in the bedroom window looking out at the street. It's still snowing. I see the streetlights dim, for a moment some vague tube inside glows orange-pink, and then the light goes out. The sun is up now. I hear the front door open and quietly close. Lyle knocks his boots against the wall. I hear him sigh as he bends to untie his laces. I hear him drop his sheepskin coat on the banister and hear it fall to the floor. I can tell he's mildly drunk. I can tell by the squeak of the banister that he's leaning on it too heavily. Finally he comes into the room behind me. I turn and I have Pete in my arms.

I say, He's asleep.

Close Your Eyes

We are on a yacht in St. Pierre. Maureen's boyfriend, Antoine, has invited us to go sailing, but there's something wrong with the engine, so we remain tied to the dock. The marina is a blast of white sails and the blue is very blue. We lie on the deck and suntan. I have a book by Marguerite Duras open on my stomach. Maureen and I read most of this book one night three years ago. A short novel about a seventy-six-year-old woman of great literary fame who attracts a thirty-six-year-old lover.

We read it in the kitchen on Gower Street during a snow-storm, taking turns reading aloud while the headlights of fishtailing cars swept the ceiling and the velvet funk of pea soup rose from the stove. We were overjoyed for Marguerite Duras. Way to go Marguerite, we yelled.

But now, three years later, the story seems very different than I remember. The young lover is bisexual. Has affairs with bartenders in a nearby hotel. He seems to be terrorizing the novelist, who is too old and proud and drunk to do anything about it. She spends all her money on him and waits for him to bring food, sometimes going hungry. How had we mistaken this for hope?

I'm also hungry. We spent a lot of money at a local shop, but most of the food has been eaten. There is a florid pink sausage pebbled with lard, and a can of duck. A package of biscuits from Norway that hasn't been opened. We're too lazy to go back into town. For a long time nobody talks. Then my husband lifts his head from a faded canvas pillow and looks one way, then the other. He puts his head back down, rolls his shoulders.

He says, I've just had a very strong memory of a bus ride in Cuba.

I say, With the careening eagle in the ravine.

He says, Not that bus ride.

I say Maureen's name. She doesn't move. Then, very slowly, she sits up. She says, Isn't sleep strange, it overtakes us all, whole cities — the activities just stop for hours. It's just struck me.

Think of all the dead people, I say.

Antoine's hand emerges from a hatch, waving a baguette. Then his head appears very near Maureen's thigh. He bites her and she squeals. He beats her stomach with the baguette.

We eat the Norwegian biscuits and dip the hardened bread in cardamom tea in enamel cups, without saying much. The fresh air has made us all sleepy. For a while, there's commotion as a giant yacht ties up next to Antoine's.

The three sailors are dressed in Helly Hanson fleece, royal blue, red, yellow. A woman of perhaps forty with a long mane of steely ringlets raises the American flag. The flag flutters weakly and then wraps itself around the mast, like a barber's pole. A white Styrofoam plate lifts itself off their deck and floats in the water. They each pause and look at it. Then they step over the deck of Antoine's yacht to get to the wharf.

As he steps from Antoine's deck, one of the Americans loses his shoe. Maureen tries to fish it out with a long pole, but the shoe begins to fill with water. Antoine climbs over the side. He inches his back down the creosote timber of the wharf with his feet jammed against the yacht. It looks like he will either be crushed or fall into the filthy harbour. A speedboat passes and the yacht moves closer and the space for Antoine is very narrow. The American woman in white pants clutches the arm of the elderly man. The man removes a white baseball cap and rubs his forehead with the back of his hand. Maureen smokes and her hand trembles near her mouth.

All this for a shoe, the man says.

But Antoine scrabbles up, spider-like, and holds the shoe in the air like a trophy. He does a little bow and tips the shoe, letting the water spill out. Everyone applauds.

Early in the morning I go to the yacht club to shower. I meet a woman and child from France, a family who tied their catamaran onto the Americans' yacht during the night. The woman gets out of the shower and isn't in a hurry to cover up. She has a tattoo of an orange and black butterfly in the concave dip near her hipbone. She scrubs her daughter with a thick white towel. The room is full of steam and the smell of shampoo. The child has the same blond hair as her mother, shiny and pale like mashed banana. The woman tells me she has been on the catamaran for five years. They have been all over the world. Both the children were born while they travelled.

When will you stop, I ask.

We will continue for a long time, she says.

Maureen wears her sunglasses. We have finished the Norwegian biscuits. In the big black lenses of Maureen's sunglasses the ropes and booms and masts all crisscross like a cat's cradle. She is crying and the tears slide down her cheeks and hang on her chin. I can't get a straight answer out of her. She has her arms wrapped around her knees. I sit up on one elbow and wave the Duras novel at her.

I say, This is nothing like what we thought.

She turns and the sun, which is setting, catches in one lens of her sunglasses and it burns a dark piercing amber and she ducks her head and puts her hand over her eyes.

She says, I wanted you to see this life.

It's foggy the day we leave. My husband shoots a video of Antoine on the dock as the ferry pulls away. He is wearing a navy and white striped T-shirt like a real Frenchman. He waves, and does not stop waving until he is engulfed by the fog.

Maureen and I met him in a bar last summer. He was wearing a faded fluorescent pink undershirt. He has an orange beard, tufts of orange under his arms, and a long orange braid.

He told us that his granny, on her deathbed, made him promise never to cut his hair.

Why would she do such a thing?

So I would understand the weight of a promise.

We watch him climb the rigging. His bare feet curling over the skeleton of the sails, a great height over the deck. His wiry body a part of the spare geometry.

Antoine's brother visits Newfoundland from Nigeria, where he's been studying giraffes and getting his pilot's license.

He raps the brass knocker on the front door and steps inside. Sunlight flashes under his arms and between his legs and the door closes and the hall is dark. He stands, not moving. I am in the kitchen with my hands in the sink. I walk down the hall to greet him. He's wearing a straw hat with tiny brass bells on the rim and patterns woven in wine and dark green straw. His face is so like Antoine's that for a moment I think it is Antoine, playing a joke. I hold out my hand, he grips it, soapsuds squish through my fingers.

Any brother of Antoine's is a brother of mine, I say. He tilts his head quizzically, and the bells jingle through the empty house.

He sleeps in the living room on the couch. There's a French door with no curtain and he sleeps in his briefs with the blankets kicked away. He finally gets up and I don't know what to do with him. With Antoine, misunderstandings could keep us talking for hours, but this guy has a firm grip on English and I'm at a loss.

Okay, stay still, I say. I'm going to paint you.

His knife pauses over the bread. A gob of marmalade hangs along the serrated edge. I do portraits in ink on wet paper. The thing about ink, as soon as you touch the brush to paper you have decided the course of the drawing. First, I am looking into his eyes. I am thinking about the shape of the eyeball, and the size, how far the eye sinks into the face. How the shadow slopes over the bone of the brow — if he sits back even an inch, the shadow will be radically different. Then the colour of his eyes startles me. I thought they were dark brown, but in this light there is a tawny copper underneath, like the bottle of marmalade, which the sun strikes so it seems to pulse. He has just come from Nigeria, and how far away that is, and what he has seen. Then I realize that I have been staring with an unself-conscious intensity into a stranger's eyes. And this brother of Antoine is staring at me and we become aware of ourselves, and the intimacy is briefly but fiercely embarrassing.

He says, gesturing to the sketchbook, Forgive me, it's my first time.

Weeks later in our kitchen I say, Antoine seemed strange to me. That weekend in St. Pierre I marked a change in him.

Late at night Maureen watched the video again and in the morning she said it was true. He had behaved differently.

I said, But he's hardly in the video at all, you can't go by that. There's a close-up of everyone playing pool. I tried to make it like John Cassevetes, swaying the camera around them, close-ups on laughing mouths, sultry eyes, chalking the pool cue. The high-pitched scrudge of chalk and cue. The camera swings around the bar and when it passes the open doorway a blast of sunshine casts a trail over the last half of the shot. A flame of blue light, an afterimage, swims briefly over the bartender and leaves a halo on Antoine's white shirt.

She's sitting on the sill of the kitchen window, a cheek and a half hefted out, so she can smoke. She turns and blows into the garden and turns back.

She says, What do you think of that? He wants to sleep with other women.

She jumps down.

Maybe I could enjoy it, she says. She holds her cigarette under the tap. I can see a tremor in her hand. Freedom, she says.

Once when we were fighting Maureen grabbed my face and kissed me on the cheek. I told her never to touch my face when I'm angry. I ran up the stairs two at a time and she was at the bottom. I leaned over the rail to shout at her, Don't touch me.

She grabbed the banister. I'll kiss you if I want, she said. Normally we never touch, we aren't touchy-feely.

I'll kiss you if I want, she screamed, the spiteful squeak of her hand on the banister. It was true, there wasn't a whole lot I could do about it.

She slammed the kitchen door. Then she opened it and said, I'm sorry, that was over the top.

Antoine tells me that if he kissed me it would be very different.

From what, I say.

From the way other men have kissed you all your life.

I say, Yes, I know. French-kissing. We have that here, too. No big deal.

He says he isn't talking about just the tongues. He says speaking French uses a whole different set of muscles in the lips, the tongue, the mouth. A kiss is different.

But you're speaking English now, I say, you probably have your technique all fucked up.

At night he comes to Maureen with something on a fork, his hand cupped underneath. The yacht is rocking gently and the fog is already settling. He says, Ferme les yeux, ouvre la bouche.

She giggles.

What is it, she says.

You must trust me, he says.

She closes her eyes and opens her mouth. She chews once, twice. And he says, a snail.

Then she screams and spits it into her hand.

Maureen says of the woman with the blonde hair like mashed banana, A life defined solely by pleasure.

I say, Yuck.

Once Maureen held a big light for Antoine when they were trying to dock at night and he said, Get it out of my fucking eyes. It was their only fight in two months of sailing.

But he was proving himself, she says, and I could have blinded him.

She looks far away, her eyes so full of the dock and him reaching for the boat, him in the brilliant blast of light and a dark, uninhabited coastline behind him.

She says, That light. And she shakes her head in amazement. Get it out of my fucking eyes, she says.

It was so heavy. It was all I could do to hold it.

After she left for France I found a diary of hers on a high cupboard shelf where we kept linen. I was alone in the house, standing on a chair gripping the dusty book. I let the diary fall open and read just one paragraph. She described a gold dress.

I snapped it shut. It was as if she were in the room, but I could feel the longing for her too — how much I missed her. The dress was a metallic orange, shiny, formfitting to just above the knee, and she wore it dancing. We went out and got drunk, walked home in a windstorm when the bars closed. There was a sluice of yellow leaves in the centre of Cathedral Street. We walked up the steep hill with our calves aching and the wet leaves clinging to our boots like spurs.

Azalea

The doorbell rings and Bethany lets herself in. She's wearing a red blazer and navy skirt. Coming from early morning mass.

Leaves fly in behind her, scrabbling sideways across the linoleum.

Trigger leaps off the kitchen chair and shoots down the hall, hitting the back of Sara's knees, slopping coffee, yelping, thrashing his tail against the coatrack.

The street behind Bethany is shiny, bluish after the rain. How bright. A boy on a bike, working hard, sun melting the chrome beneath him, obliterating spokes, the wheels flimsy as snowflakes. Flock of pigeons. An armful of flung bread crusts. A man with a stolen shopping cart, jitterbugging bottles and cans.

Bethany gives her red jacket a sharp tug, her eyes adjust to the dark hallway. Water drips on her from the ceiling.

Several drops hit her thick, grey hair imperceptibly until a single icy drop runs down the side of her face, startling her. The

church was quiet and dark. Seagulls flew over the skylight.
Father Ryan raised the Eucharist, torpid complaint from the
organ, seagulls screeching, wings slicing the pillar of sun from
the skylight. His bald head.

Now this chilly drip. She touches her cheek. Doesn't know
herself. How dark in here, cool. A deluge, part of her dream last
night. Everything comes true.

That bathtub should be fixed, Bethany says. They won't fix
anything. Peanut butter fingerprints on the French doors, dog
hair. Dust on the light fixture, cobwebs. If they'd just listen.

Sara catches a glimpse of the trees in the churchyard over
Bethany's shoulder. Big holey sponges sopping up the spill of
sunshine, outrageous orange.

There's my little boy!

Bethany crouches, twisting on her ankles, one heel lifts from
her shoe, a frost of stocking. Thomas starts down the hall,
laughing.

The arch of Bethany's foot. Stretching and exposed in
shimmery nylon. Sara imagines her as a girl. Grant McCarthy
overcoming shyness. A Knights of Columbus dance before
Grant went to war in Korea. The photograph near Bethany's
bed. Her dress with satin shoulders, frothy skirt. Her hair is so
dark it must be black, and curls, high French cheekbones.
Maybe some Mi'kmaq, the dark tan in summer. She's saucy
and adoring.

Her arms around Grant's neck, one of his hands on her
waist. Looking into each other's eyes. Coming to an understanding, there in the photograph. From here they will have six

children, call to each other from different rooms over the vacuum. A station wagon, the beach. She will go to mass. They'll lose little Davy, see his red inflatable dinosaur dipping, rising. The Atlantic roughed up farther out. Bell Island, smoky blue, windows flashing. Grabbing strangers. Have you seen? About this high. But he's safe in the car. Laughter. Fell asleep. Laughter. But the inflatable dinosaur so far out. Asleep under the sweaters. They will both agree there is a place for everything. She will put banana in the blender. He will call to her from the basement, hand resting on the banister, head bent, listening. They will come into a windfall. He touches the fork, the knife, the fringe of the placemat, waiting. A glass of milk. A linen napkin. She serves him. He thanks her. He listens to her. She tells him. They change the wallpaper, she wants it changed so they change it. Wainscotting she wants, new linoleum. They both agree to do everything. They will do everything for the children. He does the crossword. He stands for a last moment before the TV. She will want a fire. He's leaning on the rake, wipes his forehead. The water tasting of sun-warmed rubber, cut grass, and brass from the nozzle. Is it brass? He turns on the sprinkler. They will work hard but enjoy it. The children will come with the snowblower. He lights the fire. Father Ryan. Grandchildren. A drop of water, the seagulls.

This is the content of the photograph by Bethany's bed: her hands on his neck, a swing band, the glint of a horn, the crowded dance floor, an unfurling streamer.

The picture is a quiet one. The picture is a vow.

Come to Nanny, says Bethany.

Thomas holds his arms out for balance, two pale blue mitts hanging on a bit of string from the cuffs of his snowsuit. He plunges, new shoes making sharp, triumphant smacks with each step. He dives into her arms, his cheek against her chest. Her raised heel slips back in the shoe.

Why don't you do something about that leak?

She scoops Thomas up, shutting her eyes and pressing her nose to his red corduroy chest.

Nanny's going to eat you.

She wets her fingers and flicks his filmy blond hair. His cheek, a tiny imprint of an anchor from the white plastic sailor button on her blouse. Thomas grabs her gold earring and she pries his fingers away.

He always goes for the earrings.

Sara kisses Bethany's cheek. She loves her mother-in-law, there is no question. Happy birthday, Bethany. She holds out an azalea in cranberry and silver foil. The foil flings shards of reflected sunlight into Bethany's face, over the walls. The shards turn and swim like goldfish in a bowl.

I told you, says Bethany. I didn't want you to spend your money.

To replace the one.

I'm bringing it back. You shouldn't have.

Try to enjoy it!

Sara lugs Thomas's gear out to the car. Penaten, Tempra, sippy cup, the royal blue Osh Kosh. The wind plows up New Gower, the leaves, a hamburger wrapper. Sherry O'Rourke in her lime green hat waves her purse before getting on the bus.

Bethany thinks royal blue is Thomas's colour.

When Sara gets back inside, slamming the door against the wind, Bethany has set the plant on the coffee table and is standing back.

I can't accept that.

Please.

It's not a good plant.

What do you mean?

The flowers are open.

I want to —

That plant is finished.

Sara picks up the plant and whisks it out the door. She'll go for a run around the lake. Or work on the proposal. These few hours —

Bethany takes Thomas often. Then her back gives. She's resolute, pushing Thomas's stroller, every weather. She and Thomas. The park with stale bread. The beaks, angry wings, afternoon fog. If Thomas falls asleep in the fresh air.

You should see the colour in his cheeks, Bethany tells her on the phone.

Sara stands in her own kitchen. An old mattress against the back fence, yellow leaves. A cat with a patch of fur missing steps along the tops of the pickets. Bethany's garden has the glossy rhododendron. The grass sliding from dark blue to emerald to fire green, glass wind chimes.

Are you sure he's warm?

You should see!

Thomas sleeps under an afternoon sky as dark as boiling

jam, the moon, school children running along the sidewalk with their hair flying out before them, spiralling leaves, the wind thrumming the hood of Thomas's stroller.

Sara puts the azalea in the back seat of Bethany's car. New leather and tweed. She puts Thomas in the car seat and stands back. Bethany catches Sara's sleeve through her open window.

That plant is half dead.

The seatbelt locks around Bethany as she speaks, moving with an almost unnoticeable whir. The elegant motion of the automatic seatbelt stirs Sara with its prudent luxury. This is Bethany: maven steeliness. Six children, a consulting firm, St. John's, winter visits to Florida. She keeps everything immaculate. Indecent to pay for something she's able to do herself. She will always take care of her own house. She likes gadgets, a long-handled lint remover, a grill that drains fat, a silver toast holder. But there's no clutter. She and Grant haven't succumbed to greed or any kind of eccentric frugality. They've worked steadily, been generous and careful.

The seatbelt rolls into place.

Thomas behind the window. The reflections of clapboard, telephone pole, tree branches swipe sideways, Sara's own face leaning in, obscuring him, then his hand on the glass. Little smack she hears. Pale palm. Bethany pulls away and then Sara runs to catch the phone.

She's holding a chocolate chip cookie in one hand, listening.

She's facing the kitchen window, the rain has begun. The mattress, the cat. If a black cat is bad luck, what about a white cat? Where are Thomas and Bethany now? The stoplight near Don Cherry's Sports Grill? The rain leaves long, thin marks like sewing needles on the window. Butter she made these cookies with, his little hand in the sliding branches. She holds the receiver.

Dave says, I got the job in Montreal.

What Sara knows: They aren't as sophisticated as she thought. He is this; she is that. They are an invention of randomness. Relationship as lackadaisical conspiracy against. Against what? A situation not entirely without romance. But bracing, a hail-storm, a do-si-do on black ice.

The farmer's market. Bethany always says about the carrots. Thomas loves them with table butter. A little table butter. Go to the farmer's market, everything there is so sweet!

Bethany names the things that matter in life: a coddled egg, boiled wool, fresh sheets, doeskin gloves, ironed shirts, old-fashioned beans, table butter, the farmer's market.

The woman behind the vegetable counter, her breath hanging in the air. She wears a South American cap that comes down over her ears, the strings untied, gloves without fingers. Sara takes carrots and potatoes, a bag of brussels sprouts. Dave doesn't like them. He goes, But you buy it if you like them. Just because I don't, doesn't mean.

She never does. She never buys the things he doesn't like. She does this time. She wants the crenellated density, the fierce bunchiness, the dank green of a brussels sprout. He doesn't get to. He always. She has never. Bacon, liver, raw mushrooms, the stalks of romaine lettuce, these are the things she's given up for him.

She wants the organs, things that root.

She wants a chicken dinner, raisins and garlic in the dressing. A pumpkin with an emergency candle. The smell of roasting yams.

Sunlight strikes the jars of bakeapples and she wants to buy them just for the colour.

James Anderson. She remembers too late, Jim. She had been calling him Jim for the last two years.

Mr. Anderson.

Sara.

The whites of his eyes are yellow, almost mustard, and his lashes are crusted with a medication, something leaking. A new, dramatic frailty.

They ate together in the summer room. She was teaching him to cook. They sat at a glass and chrome table. A giant window that looked onto his late wife's rose garden. All the bushes were wrapped in burlap, wearing caps of snow. As the late afternoon turned into evening the window became black and reflected the two of them. Three floating candle flames. James's white hair.

Are you still willing to move to Montreal, Dave asks.

A housefly caught between the kitchen windowpanes. The cat on the fence flicks its ear, the mattress. The fly hyper-vivid, rubbing its forelegs together, one on top of the other, then switching, so the alternate leg is on top. The fridge cuts in. Such steadfastness, the absorbing industry. She takes a bite of the cookie. Yesterday she had wanted to. What had it been? Jayne had invited Nancy but had left Sara out. She'd felt the supreme effort that casual intimacy exacts. The strangling network of her social life, these inadvertent slights. She'd crushed the paper coffee cup. Dave was already home when she got there. Before she had taken off her coat, he told her he wanted to leave. Imagine a city, he'd said. She had said, Let's do it. I want to go too.

Your eyes, she says.

I'm having an operation.

The bakeapples flare and flare and flare. The traffic. People turning on their lights. Dusk. Sara hasn't seen Mr. Anderson since Thomas's birth. He'd dropped off a sleeper, but Dave had got the door. She couldn't get up. She'd hardly left the bed. The weepy hours. Watching old movies. Every Paul Newman. Snow falling over the street, the car roofs, the branches. Accumulating silently, with diligence, covering the black, wet branches, floating against the grey dusk, under the streetlights, and finally against the blue-black sky. Waiting to hear Dave on the front steps, his key, the door. Hardly getting up. Paul Newman. Holding out his broken thumbs. Weeping over Paul Newman's. His eyes. His thumbs. They broke his thumbs in one movie. It had begun to snow in St. John's, and her milk had come in. Her milk and the snow. Dave was working. Weeping because St. John's, the Narrows, the snow. Someone brought a stew and she cried with gratitude.

She met with James's daughter. They'd known each other at the university. Emily and her new lover. Left his wife. Though it was the first time Sara had met him, she had the impression the ordeal had changed his face overnight. The face of a man who had altered his course. Emily drinking. They had been to see a play. About an affair. Wasn't it about an affair, darling? A suffering wife. Didn't you think? But you don't.

The boyfriend rubs his eyes with his fists. A deliberate gesture, a sidewalk mime or caged ape indicating spiritual exhaustion.

It takes an incredible will to do the right thing, he says. Everybody must try. The courage you must summon.

It just didn't have a very satisfying ending, says Emily, that's my feeling. I wanted it one way or the other. Isn't that what you ask of a play? One way or the other? If I'd wanted shiftless ambiguity I could have stayed home.

Sara tried to remember what the man did for a living. Was it anything that would equip him? Did they have a car nearby at least?

It's very taxing being the world's biggest bitch, Emily says. She giggles.

Then she touches Sara's hand.

Stay away from my father, Sara, she says. Don't let him become —

Become what?

A lech.

You've got it all wrong.

Just listen to me.

Rain hits the kitchen window and Sara sees the garden behind the housefly. The fly is lost forever; the garden is alive with rain and colour. An orange towel fell off the line a long time ago and no one has bothered to do anything. It's half-covered with leaves. In the opposite garden there's a statue of the Buddha with the gold paint coming off, the white plaster visible beneath.

You go to Montreal, she says. I'll decide later.

What are you talking about, Dave says.

He can go. She might stay on. It sends a ticklish flutter, just the thought. The cookie is so good. The table butter is Bethany's influence.

The vegetables come right out of the ground, Bethany says, no sprays or pesticides, nothing like that. Mash them in a little bowl with table butter.

James is seventy. Sara cooked the most exotic things. Recipes off the Internet. She had never attempted these dishes before. He insisted on paying for the food and wine.

Once, to surprise her, he'd had a small jar of truffles imported from Italy. They took a truffle out of the little jar, there were five in all. It lay on the cutting board. James bowed, his hands clasped behind his back, almost touching it with his nose.

My God, he'd said. Smell it.

She'd leaned in and done the same. It was earthy, of course, but she imagined she was smelling something else. Whatever made the pigs dig for it. It went through her, a tingling in her belly, she felt it between her legs. Then she straightened up, blushing. She asked what he thought of Emily's married lover. The question was too personal, she was slightly drunk, but there was no way to retract it.

I want my daughter to feel passion, at any cost. A terrible thing for a father.

He picked up the truffle and bit it. He held the other half out for Sara. She opened her mouth and he put it in, his thumb resting on her lip.

She read later that one truffle will flavour a whole meal.

Sara hadn't returned either of James's two phone messages after the baby. The summer. A waterfall. The beach, a bicycle. Crabapples, kerosene lamps, rainstorms, the whales. Her bare feet on the dash, a take-out coffee. Dave driving. Dave's black curly hair, a dark tan. A ball of earwigs falling from the cupboard onto the shelf, a jar of rusted screws. Three Rottweilers swimming through the long grass like eels. She had just enough time to scoop up the baby and run inside. The hammock, smoothing massage oil on Dave's shoulders, his stomach, his thighs. The oil smelled of cinnamon and orange rind, the bottle said castor, sweet almonds, coconut. It got in her hair and the smell gave her dreams of furtive sex in jungles and sand dunes, a hothouse. She made Dave wake up.

The woman behind the vegetable counter handed her change and she jammed it into her pocket. The wind blew from behind James, his white hair, his scarf.

My eyes are giving me trouble.

We wouldn't have to eat.

You weren't around for so long.

I was busy. I was tired.

You had the baby to think about.

Weeping all the time. I watched so much Paul Newman. There was so much snow.

Last winter.

After the baby.

The cat springs into an overhanging branch. The branch wags violently. Two sparrows rise up, fly over the Buddha. The rain is harder now. The fly is inert. It may have died there. She sees the wings are dusty. It's covered in a webbing. Had she imagined its legs rubbing together? It's been dead for years.

You'd leave me, Dave asks.

Anything can happen, she says.

She's late for Thomas, but only by a few minutes. Bethany is spinning a saucepan lid on the floor before him. Sara struggles to get him in his snowsuit. She kisses his face all over. She tastes banana in his hair.

Passes the living room on her way out. Bethany has just had it painted a dark gold. They've changed the wallpaper. Then Sara notices the azalea. The buds are closed tight.

Sara feels a glittery stomach-swirling foreknowledge.

How can that be?

Oh, I returned the one you gave me, Bethany says. This one hasn't bloomed yet.

If You're There

I am waiting for Jeremy to show on his bike. I sit on the patio of Future Bakery waiting for him. Chilly, still. No leaves. But everybody, the bikes, a skirt flapping back off a thigh, the army boot touching down, a full stop. Red light, the bicycle. He'll come around the corner. The cars are splats, blue, red, blooming and contracting in the big wall of glass beside me. Zoom. The girl on the bike, flicking through, gone. There he is, take him in. Take his measure.

A shirt, some snazzy thing he's got on. We never hug; I hug him. Because I decided to. I'm starting to feel my age. A nostalgia for things that haven't happened yet. Or they've happened at such a velocity that I'm left behind, still waiting for them. Anticipation so heightened it makes my funny bone ring. I'm going to hug Jeremy from now on, every time I see him. I'm never going to not hug. Not just him, everybody. A new me, a hugging me.

I came to Toronto because I hadn't seen Lily and Marco for so long, because I had some money, to get away from the baby, drink coffee at Lily's kitchen table, eat things. Fusion. Maybe get drunk. For a long time you couldn't get shiitake mushrooms in St. John's. Lemongrass we have. I wanted to see Jeremy. I haven't seen him since he left Newfoundland two years ago. He's come into some serious money and I think he might disappear with it.

Lily and I met at art school centuries ago. She's got some new grey at the temples; other than that she's exactly the same. They're both the same, Lily and Marco, but why did I let five years go by? I need her. The way she knocks foreheads with the cat.

Lily says, I want to crack the new painting wide open. Her painting in the centre of the living room, some bare canvas still showing, the spotlight with a crush of tinfoil over the rim focussing the beam. The rest of the room is darkish, even in the morning. A quiet street, you can see the squirrels leaping, silhouettes, the branches thrashing briefly. The cavernous sofa that Lily's recovered in velvet. A Graham Coughtry, two figures interlocked, just a few sure, dangerous lines of ink.

Often she sits for an hour or more in front of the painting, her back very straight, smoking. I've seen her drip gold from a tiny bottle. I stand behind her with my coffee. Blues, pinks, lemon, almost white in the centre, all of it in motion, sunlight on water.

It's still representational, she says. One minute it's brushstrokes and colour, the next minute —

She's taking me to her Improv Contact class. I'm nervous. Look, she says, it'll be fine.

Walking there, the crocuses. Spring on Yonge, smart and awake, like toothpaste. We cross the bridge and into the subway station, warm uprush, vaguely feculent: feet, newsprint, grease. Lily drops two tokens. She's wearing a jacket I've never seen before, unholy pink. Her glasses on a string. Glasses she didn't have the last time I was here.

She and Marco hardly touch breakfast but she makes us cappuccino first thing, the whistling, hacking steam. The cappuccino maker is new. All the cats. Last year she coaxed a feral kitten by lying on her stomach in the backyard for a full week, extending a stick with a gob of wet food on the end. She stops halfway down the stairs to the trains. Stands still.

I need a can of house paint, she says, I'll pour it. A few subway transfers lift in a subterranean wind and eddy around her knees. She trots down the stairs again and I hurry to catch up.

This Contact thingy, I say. Do they talk, at Contact?

Roar of train, she closes her eyes against it.

There's little talk, she says.

So you just approach someone?

You sidle up.

And touch them?

You'll see. It's very sweet.

A church basement, no music. Everyone wearing sweats. A woman rolls toward me. Her bare foot squeaks on the gym floor. I'm lying on my stomach. Old wood, shiny brown varnish. High ceilings.

My first time, I whisper.

Mine too.

Our calves touch, we start like that. Her ankle looks stern, circumspect. Her ankle looks like the right-sized wrench grasping a bolt. This is a stranger's ankle. An ankle that has come from somewhere: an old-fashioned bathtub with a flare of rust near the drain, plume of leftover, slow-breaking bubbles, red sock, a streetcar, she's stepping off and pigeons fly up, just bones. I'm loving that I'll never see her again. So few people do I never see again. Our thighs, the backs of our hands, touching. One shoulder, the other. I'll see Jeremy later, tomorrow. He has an answering machine, the old kind, with a tape.

I say, If you're there. It's me. Jem, if you're there? But he doesn't pick up. I listen to the oceanic silence in the pay phone receiver, a phone on Bloor, it's sunny, someone opens a glass door and the world in the glass folds into spears of light and flings itself wide open again, cars emerge, skyscrapers, a woman it takes a beat to recognize, slightly elongated, the camel-hair coat, myself. I believe Jeremy's listening to my voice in the empty room. I imagine him sitting in a chair, the fabric worn shiny and torn at the armrest, burlap and coarse cotton batting with flecks of sawdust poking through. Some chair he dragged in from outside, a shawl thrown over the back. His hands in his hair. Listening, yawning, the kettle plugged in.

Jeremy? Pick up. I know you're there.

I roll on top of her, her bum. Imagine, in a city this big, the swimming pools from the air, trees, warehouses. My hipbone in the cleft of her bum, and rolling away, our feet locked. Just toes. You don't not touch, you touch. Lily has assured me there's nothing sexual about Contact.

It's not that way, she says. It just isn't. There was a notice to that effect a couple of weeks ago. I can't remember how it was worded.

I'd love to know, I say.

It was the gist, says Lily.

Worded. Nothing exists until it's worded. How deliberate it all is: this ankle, my marriage, the baby, Jeremy's bike locked to a post somewhere. The money he's made, suitcases, Europe he's saying. Australia. He's not really saying. The way he will thread through a crowd the last time I see him, turn a corner. My voice in an empty room. I believe it is empty after all. Listen, if you're there.

Our spines, this stranger's and mine, touching like the inner workings, the cogs of something precious: a Swiss watch, a bank safe. My head drops into the curve of her neck. She squishes herself under me. Lifts. The end of her ponytail against my cheek. Her body as spare and emphatic as a jungle gym. Then I dance with a man who has sweat dripping from his face. It drips from his hair, his eyebrow, the tip of his nose. He wears drawstring pants and rising from the waistband is a swirl of black hair up his belly. He thrusts me skyward with one hand. My thigh pressing his damp neck.

Jeremy has broken up with Stella. Stella calls me in St. John's and we talk for hours. We have talked this way since grade ten. I've got the yellow tablecloth under my elbows. A white bowl with a mottled banana and a paperclip, the pip of an orange. The baby is asleep, my husband has gone upstairs to write. He's writing a sociology of hell. He just showed me a picture of a monster eating people and shitting them out whole. A screaming, kicking person in each of the monster's hands, another coming out the monster's anus. Horned angels piggy-backing naked sinners, dropping them through the clouds into the tortured throngs below. The caption says, An example of Renaissance overcrowding. He hands me a joint. It takes only one stretchy moment to feel stoned. I must make sense. I sit up straight, a nimble recruit in the war for adroit thought.

He says, If you watered the plants now and then you might have some appreciation for them. The phone rings. Stella, calling from Toronto.

She says, I wake up, my heart is racing.

Listen. If you want him back bad enough.

I do.

If you want him back, you go get him.

And I like, what, hit him over the head with a club?

Just coat the guy with snot and tears.

Snot, she says.

You weep and beg and cover him with snot, drip all over him. I believe any woman can get any man, I say.

The statement leaves me giddy, exhausts me. I wonder, during the ensuing silence, if I believe it. I find that I do, though I also know it to be, in some minor way, incorrect.

I've tried that, Stella says. There's another silence.

I've tried snot, she says.

More snot, I say. Just go with more snot.

After Contact, Lily and I sit at an old picnic table outside the church, facing a chainlink fence, a parking lot. Ukrainian hymns come through the brick. Lily lights a cigarette.

I like to sit here after, she says, and just —

She takes a deep draw on her cigarette. We're in the shade and the smoke looks blue and hangs. There's no hurry. Lily has always been beautiful. Right now she's very beautiful. My husband stirring something with his hand in a stainless steel bowl the night before I got on the plane. That hour after the dishes, the baby asleep.

The kitchen echoing itself, concentric rings of kitchen pulsing from the kitchen. This would be the moment my husband and I have worked toward all day, every day, for fourteen years, more or less. The dryer going. The kettle. The rest of the house detaching like the burnt-out parts of a rocket.

It was potatoes, he was pouring a dressing. Tapping the paprika jar with his finger, clouds of it sifting. The potatoes falling through his fingers against the bowl. He held his hand, shiny with oil, under the tap. Flicked his hand a couple of times, dried it with the tea towel. I knew he would say about the floor. About the floor would be the next thing. He covered the bowl with plastic wrap and put it in the fridge. He opened the paper. Look at that, he said. The phone rang and neither of us moved. Can you believe it, he said and turned the page.

I see *The New Yorker* lying in the breadbasket. A story it's taking me two days to read. A boy and his father, ducks. So rich that Louisiana came over me in the supermarket, and I've never even been there. Later, while putting clothes in the dryer, I imagined the smell of swamps. Last night I'd crept down the stairs into the cold kitchen, my T-shirt and underwear, looking for *The New Yorker* to finish the story. Wanting the climax, resolution. Gunshots. The boy and his dad, unyielding loss. Wanting to read myself to sleep. But when I got to the kitchen I couldn't remember why I was there. Now, in the breadbasket.

This floor, my husband says. He turns the page.

In the shady alley outside Contact, lightly perspiring, all of that comes to me: the kitchen, the way the lamp over the fridge caught my husband's freckles. And from nowhere, walking home with him from a bar the first night we slept together. He lit a candle and that was the only light. I was wearing a cotton dress that got twisted so that I couldn't move under the heavy bedclothes, woollen tights. We had come in from the rain and the candlelight in his black hair, his lower lip gleaming, his earlobe was dark and, when I touched it, hot. How he convinced me.

The scene doesn't unfold, but manifests of a piece, truer than the chainlink fence, Lily's pink jacket, the Ukrainian hymns through the brick. Truer. I am of an age. Things are passing through me. Ungraspable. And gone. Not memory, it barely has content. Some story in *The New Yorker*, the yellow tablecloth. Is/was. But my skin gets goose bumps that I recognize as or confuse for love, amorphous, rough-hewn. My husband in the replenishing kitchen. From a time long past: two days ago.

Lily is talking about her brushstrokes, some flying up to the surface and just as quickly receding. I see the paintings. The one with the darkness closing in is about giving birth. Paprika. Turning off the tap, flicking his hand. The tea towel.

You're going to hate me, I say. She drops the cigarette and steps on it. Okay, I know this is crass, but the painting over the sofa is vaginal to me. Like when I gave birth, that painting is.

I don't hate you, she says. She pats my back. All the paintings are like *coming*.

Jeremy has moved out, rented a small room of his own before he takes off for Europe. I have the perverse desire to tell him what to do. Jeremy has become impregnable, ephemeral. I can't get a reading. Before now, I thought myself an excellent judge of character, gifted in this regard. Now, however, I don't believe people have characters. I believe it's something we impose on their actions in retrospect, a mirage. He is this way, that way. (My husband evaporates. I'm in Toronto! This is what I am in a parallel world, a woman in a camel-hair coat, fresh from a dance class. Someone has hung a perfectly good leather jacket on a fence post. I might take it, nobody knows me.)

I want to tell Jeremy this: We come apart.

But that's no newsflash. Everybody knows we come apart. That's why we cling so desperately. I slapped *The New Yorker* down and got the bucket and the mop. Yes, I'm doing the goddamn floor, okay. There, the floor. Are you happy?

The wide street at the end of the alley is blaring with sunlight. A car goes past with a radio and is gone.

We'll walk, Lily says. She draws her knees up, rests her chin. She's petite. Watching her dance at Contact, like putting your thumb against the bristles of a brush, flicking paint. The way she tosses her head, her arching back. Her fingers. In a minute we'll walk, she says.

You're so shy, I say, this Contact thing is so.

It's about right for me, she says. It's just about my speed.

We walk along Queen and a man on crutches offers Lily daffodils. His eyes watery, knuckles on the handles, leaning forward.

I bought these for you, he says.

Let me give you some money. She has taken out a coin purse and ten dollars.

I wouldn't take a penny, he says. I couldn't take it from you. I could not. I absolutely. Those flowers are a gift. He puts the money in his pocket.

He says, What's your name?

Lily.

Lily. This money is going to Sick Kids'. That's where your money's going. I want you to know. We walk away and Lily turns and waves to him. She waves goodbye with the daffodils, and puts her face in them.

We got some flowers anyway, she says. Her nose reddens and a gleaming line of tears. But she forces her eyes wide so they don't fall and she bursts into laughter.

It's just that it could be my father. Or any one of us.

Lily. You shouldn't be allowed out.

Lily's husband, Marco, is a physics professor. I have always hugged Marco without a second thought. There's no question. There has never been a warmer guy. Sitting at his computer, halo of grey hair. Clicking. He tells me about gravity.

We don't know if it's instantaneous, or does it propagate through space like electricity. If God puts this here. He swivels in his chair and places his cup.

I say, God, but there is no God.

As you know, there is no God. We are talking about a cup. How long does it take? He slides the cup to the edge of the table and almost lets it fall. Lily gives him a piece of bread covered with butter. Puts it down on the side table. Marco stands, stretches.

Baby, he says. He takes her face in his hands.

This girl, he says, can you believe this girl?

I thought there was a given amount of matter, I say. I thought if something disappeared from this side of the world it would show up on the other side, drawn by gravity. I imagine Jeremy in Trafalgar Square, putting his suitcase down, the fountains, children with bright, unbuttoned coats, the double-decker buses. He's just standing.

Marco has already sat back down. The bread and butter will go untouched for a long time. He is almost lost to the computer. But he swivels. My ignorance bewilders him. A given amount of matter? His eyebrows, his eyes.

No, he says, this goes on all the time. Matter gets changed into energy. You didn't know?

How easy it is for me to forget the cold facts. Energy, grammar. I like it loosey-goosey. I like the fact of Marco. The fact of Lily. But mostly there are no facts worth counting on. I don't like to think someone can hug you goodbye, that he can disappear in a crowd. I don't like that people go away, or worse, I might forget them. Cling, goddamn it.

Jeremy, I'm at a pay phone on Bloor, listen, if you're there could you just —

Hellllooooo.

Jeremy. You're there.

Jeremy! He sits. I stand. We stand and I hug him. My cheek on his chest. Some snazzy shirt. If I'm going to do this hugging thing. I don't let go. That's the way they do it in Toronto. He's been up here long enough, he'll be used to it. I hug and hug. I feel all his bones, his shoulder blade. He does not pat my back in the way that means a fine, over-now-though hug. Rather, he accepts the hug expertly. Perhaps he has always been able to hug. Maybe all of my friends. The Contact dancer laying her hands on my hips and drawing me up from the floor, lifting me onto her shoulder.

I say, I thought we were getting Vietnamese.

We're not staying here?

No, I want to eat Vietnamese.

You look good. Do I? But your coffee? I'm done. It's. No. It's so great to see you. So, I'll take you. You said a place on Spadina. We said, didn't we? You do, are you good? I'm good, yes, I'm yes. But you're not good, you're sad. I'm sad, he says. I'm sad but I'm good. I'll fix you up, I say, let me tell you what I think you should do. Tell me, he says.

I never believe Jeremy's eyes are green. I believe that's an affectation he cultivates. Or in a certain light. But it's true. Today. Alive in his face. The whole street, octopus, mussels, dolls in plastic wrap. I pick up my chopsticks and he picks up his. I know him inside out and I know he doesn't know how to use chopsticks. I know him, this guy. Everything. He picks them up while looking into my eyes. He's bluffing. He picks them up without thinking. Snaps them. A man the world sparkles for, or on account of. What if something should ever happen to him? Unpeeling my forearms from the warm plastic tablecloth. The sun cuts across my neck, the blind halfway. We are the only white people.

You order for me, I say. He tells me what he's ordering. But I'm not listening, just watching him, the waiters behind, a jug of water, a woman with a lime green ribbon in her shiny, straight black hair.

Red Dragon, Dragon Star, Dragon's Claw, some fruit the name of which I can't remember. He gave me an exotic fruit for my birthday two years ago. Always something I've never tasted before. Cut it open on a wooden board, the flesh such a shocking fuchsia, so vibrant against the waxy green peel. I wouldn't eat it because I thought I was pregnant. The spikes. Passed my plate on. He was disappointed. Still, it reminded me of the beach at Cow Head, vibrant colour. The men getting out of the ocean, naked, way down the beach. The wind trying to rip away their white towels. Stella and I at the coin-operated telescope, training on a ship.

My husband yelling, Hey, get that thing away from us. Jeremy, the girls are trying to peek.

Stella yelling back, Listen you guys, looks to me like you could do with a little magnification. You know what I'm saying?

A sailor on the deck dressed in white. He raises his arm, tentative. Shimmering. The boys have walked, dressed now. They are near. I hear them, and a metal eyelid falls over the gorgeous blue. Our quarter's worth. Step back from the eyepiece. Towels around their necks. We ate lobster in the Cow Head restaurant with the big window, linen napkins. Our cheeks sunburned, sneakers full of sand. Mussels, alive, alive oh. The sun went down and the room turned vibrant red.

Things I've never tasted before. Wrapped in brown paper, dripping. What haven't I eaten, ever? Tripe. Brain. Once on a beach in Morocco with my husband and a French couple. She wore a white scarf, the wind fluttered, there was a bonfire, a bucket of fish. A table, there on the beach, a checkered cloth. The Frenchman lifted out the spine of my fish with one motion. His wife's gold earring shot out light. You will not find a single bone, the Frenchman said. As though this kind of thoroughness was exquisite. Something we could strive to achieve. I want to be that couple still, fourteen years later. I want to be French, on the beach in all that wind. Fresh fish still panting in a galvanized bucket with a skim of water, the shiny blue eye reflecting sky, cloud. The table on the sand, the sharp knife opening the fish, the gentle tugging until the spine parts from the flesh, intact. Ocean.

My husband is tall, big bones. I like the large bones, he has substance, sleeping beside me. He can ward things off. How committed he is to his sleep. The ringing chink of the weights he brings together over his chest while lying on the living-room floor. The abandon with which he flings himself into whatever he does. Hard to get along with when he's working. Peculiar about meat. His grasp. He knows everything, everything. He exhausts me. Makes me shake with anger, slobber with tears. Grey long johns he got second hand. I think, perhaps an affair in Berlin last year. Never losing his temper: he doesn't believe in it. A temper is something you choose to lose, he says. You decide. Then the extravagance with which he loses his temper: You have never watered a plant in your life, have you? Have you? Screaming: You've never watered a fucking plant in your entire life. We ate wild boar in a French village, the lavender in the fields. A big table, a dinner party, and we were looking at each other, each tasting boar for the first time. The world goes canny and alien, and you both experience it. Succulent, earthy, unnameable boar.

Your bike?

We'll leave it.

Jeremy claps his gloves in front of him. One smack.

So, how about green tea ice cream? We'll go somewhere else.

He stops on the corner of Bloor and Spadina, he seems to have lost his sense of direction entirely.

Now, we are where?

Spadina, I say. This is Spadina. And you're doing okay, I say. I make one eyeball fierce. It's the best I can do since I'm so short beside him. Give him an eyeball. I got this eye from my father. Also a short person.

The strangest thing I ever ate was with Stella. Two Panamanians once made us a grey stew with pigs' hocks, which are ankles, essentially, and a slow, bouncing, naked onion, roiling in the glass pot on the stove top. Did we sleep with them, the Panamanians? Of course we did, that was love too. Cartilage, a couple of carrots. So hot my nose, my eyes. Whatever spices they used. So hot I became new. Try that.

After the ice cream on Spadina I watch Jeremy walk into the crowd. It's the last time I will ever see him.

The Stylist

The stylist stands behind you and leans in. She scrunches your hair in her fists, testing bounce. She lifts it to the sides like wings, tugging her fingers through the snags.

She says, What's the idea here?

The idea is I want to look good.

You want a change, she says. Your husband left you. Your husband left you. Your husband left you.

Uncross your legs, she says. You adjust your posture. She spreads her hands on your shoulders, meets your eyes in the mirror.

Now listen, you'll have to sit up straight.

You have hunched since competitive diving at the Aquarena when you were twelve and grew breasts. Your bathing suit, the frosty green of the old Ford. The green of leaves covered with short silver hair, lucent grapes. You wore this bathing suit every day after school. The chlorine wearing the lycra thin, fading the sheen. When the bathing suit was wet your nipples were visible. The colour of your nipples.

You hunch your shoulders. You aren't like the older girls whose breasts are a fact.

Your breasts are tender, a rumour, the beginning of a long story, a page-turner. It's the worst when you're speaking with your coach. The bathing suit transparent as the skin of a grape you peel with your teeth.

The lineup for the ladder is the worst. Long enough for the warm lights to make the beads of water on your arms creep to a standstill, chlorine tingles your skin. Under the water nobody can see your nipples. Diving practice enchants you. You fall asleep as soon as you get home. Asleep before the soaps, drooling on the cushion. Over your fried eggs and beans, the ketchup screaming on the white plate.

This is what the table looks like: placemats with illustrations of a fox hunt. Red riding jackets, top hats, hounds. A silver water pitcher, greasy with condensation. An ashtray with a smoking cigarette. Your father's empty chair. His placemat, without the cutlery. Your mother is likely to cry. She cries every night. Sometimes while watching the news, sometimes over supper. These are her specialties: sweet-and-sour ribs with tears, spaghetti with tears, steak, baked potato, tears. Mom, hold the tears.

This is what you see out the window: hideous icicles, a row of fangs. You dream you kiss your coach.

A kiss so ripe and desperate, nothing else will ever come close.

He kisses you and cups his hand under your chin and one of your front teeth drops into his open palm. Blood seeps from the fleshy hole. You know at once it isn't a baby tooth. Now you must go through life like this. Icicles crash from the eaves.

In the morning you run your tongue and run your tongue. Your mother and you live in the mouth of winter, waterlogged. The sky is a ravenous mink, the spruce trees raking its wet fur underbelly. You have become enchanted. Your coach lifting weights in the chrome gym, wiping his glistening neck with a white towel, rolling his shoulders, sweat in his eyelashes. He lies on his back, a leg on either side of the black vinyl bench. The leg of his shorts gapes and you see the white perforated cotton inside and the bulge of his penis, pubic hair. You have never seen. This is something else. Something else again. When he stands up the foggy print of his sweat in the vinyl, his spine, his shoulder blades like the wings of a dragonfly. Rank gym, feet, the iron smell of clanking weights, chlorine, boiling hot-dogs from the hot air vent, the tangy liniment. The slap of his hand against his wet neck. The smell of his liniment. Like laundry dried in the wind and licorice, coniferous.

How fickle the water is. You slip in from a great height and the blush in your cheeks cools. The water unzippers your new-girl body, your breasts, the hunch. The water peels you. The saddest thing you've ever seen is the back of your father's green Ford raising clouds of dust that make the alders unshiny. The saddest thing is that Ford turning the corner.

Or the pool rises up in a fist and mangles your face.

A month ago you blackened both your eyes. They swelled

shut. Two plums sitting neat. Sockets like eggcups. A blow so stunning it seemed ordained. The fangs snapped shut. Mink savaging the hind leg of a cloud. Your mother kneeling near your head on the concrete.

Next we'll see the macaroni, she says.

You vomit chlorine and macaroni. Where has she come from? She was supposed to be at work. How long have you been out? She would have had to come across the city. The back of her hand on your cheek. She would have had to know without being told.

But here you are again, toes curled over the edge of the ten-metre board. It's warm up here because you're near the lights. You're in the rafters. Far away, at the other end of the Aquarena, an aerobics class.

Your coach could turn on the bubbles. No matter what, it will be okay if he turns on the bubbles, which cost money, which aren't allowed at the Nationals, which make the water as welcoming as whipped cream.

He wants to see a triple.

You want the bubbles but you don't ask. You are in love, the black Trans Am with a flame that bursts over the hood, the megaphone. He's sitting in a canvas chair by the side of the pool and he's wearing black flip-flops with red plastic flowers. He speaks to you.

Shoulders, he says. Although it's a megaphone, his tone sounds bedroomy. He calls you by your last name.

Focus Malone.

It's strange, but you are very good at diving. You are the

youngest on the provincial team. You will go to the Nationals. You have come to suspect you can do absolutely anything. It's intoxicating, this glimmer of your will. The pool crunches your ribs like a nutcracker, the board nicks your shin, unspooling a ribbon of blood in the water, a love tap on the left shoulder so you can't lift your arm.

Or the pool plays dead. It doesn't matter, you keep doing it. Doing begets doing. You could go on like this forever.

You unhunch. It's a magic trick, the triple. The action doesn't happen until it's over. It happens in the future and you catch up. A triple is déjà vu. Trusting the untrustable.

The key: give yourself over/over/over.

The stylist reams a finger around your cape collar, loosening. Takes a steel comb, flicks it against her hipbone. You are thirty-four and you've been to a stylist a handful of times. Maybe six, not ten.

She says, That length is doing nothing for you.

She whips your swivel chair: slur of mirror, porcelain, chrome, fluorescent nettles stick themselves to the glass. Droning hair dryers, running water, phones.

The stylists talk. A mazey, elliptical daisy chain of talk. They adhere to nothing. Vacation packages, electric toothbrushes, blind dates. (He's got to be kidding: *coffee*. Going for coffee equals *death*. Night skiing, spritzers, bowling, sea-kayaking, I'm like, Okay. Let's *go*. But coffee? He's kidding, right?) They are the experts on every topic. Hair is a mild distraction. Hair happens.

She flicks the steel comb and it whirs near her hip. She's drawing a conclusion.

Your hair: upkeep, damage, regrowth, definition, product, lifestyle, frost, frizz, product, streaks, foils, body, cut. Where you're a small person. Where you've got a round face.

Outside, the storm slows traffic like a narcotic. You haven't seen a winter like this since. The equipment is breaking down. Bring in the army, they're saying. At night the snowplows crash into the drifts and stagger backward like dazed prizefighters. The windshields have bushy eyebrows. Cars stuck on the hills, smoking tires, engines squealing like dolphins. You haven't seen anything like this since you were a kid. You and your mother, the icicles, the lake catching over, the wind circling the glassy trees like a wet finger tracing a crystal rim. Her sleeping pills, the alarm clock blaring near her ear. Stumbling from your room at dawn to wake her so she can drive you to diving practice. The smell of chlorine in your skin always, your hair.

You like your driveway to be scraped down to the pavement since your husband left you. You get out there early every Saturday morning. The children watch from the living-room window. Your little daughter taps the glass. She waves. Your son puts his lips against the glass in a big gummy kiss.

The hospital room zings. Your husband says he wants a smoke. His forehead is gleaming, his eyebrows raised. He's feral, acute with stillness. His hazel eyes, flecks of rust, hair white as a fresh sheet of paper. He's socking one fist gently into his open palm.

You breathe. The minute hand reverberates each time it

moves, a *twang*. You wait, wait for it, wait. The minute hand moves. Your mother lays an icy towel on your forehead. A drop of water moves down your temple and into your ear. The moving drop is exquisite in every way. The contraction recedes. The nurse is driving a spaceship in her sleep. She's gripping the arms of the chair, leaning slightly forward, snoring.

Go have your smoke, you say. Nothing's happening yet.

But it starts to happen while he's in the parking lot. He tells you later about his moment: how he will never be the same. He's standing on a slab of concrete near a loading entrance at the back of the hospital. The door is tied open with a piece of rubber tubing. The smell of cold food, sausage, powdered egg, the churning of dishwashers, spilled cutlery. It's a foggy night and he can smell the harbour and something bitter, pigeon shit. He's bewildered, hardly able to remember how he got where he is.

When he goes back to your hospital room his son's head is visible, becomes visible with each contraction and disappears again. It's the most awesome, unlovely, soul-quaking thing he has ever seen. He cups one of your heels in his hand, your mother holds your other heel. The baby is mauve coloured, smeared darkly with guck, and crying.

Your hair will be by Suzanne.

They're single or have just eloped, the stylists, young or staving off age with fashion, trend. The best one-room apartments in the city.

Do you have children, Suzanne?

Nope. No. Thank. You.

And you don't ever?

You got that right. Kids are so *expensive*. Why would you?

Suzanne knows what she doesn't want. Sometimes desire is forged by the process of elimination. Your husband wanted golfing and hockey, a new tent, to celebrate his Native heritage (hitherto unmentioned during seven years of marriage), to become a theologian, to hunt seals. (There's a white mask the Inuit hunter holds to his face while approaching the seal basking at the edge of an ice floe. Everything is white, the hunter's white furs, the ice, the air. When he lifts the white mask he's obliterated. Your husband, the empty landscape, your husband, the empty landscape.) You prefer oblique dreams but you are too tired to manufacture the oblique. He wanted to be a vegetarian. (There are foods you can't face anymore. Basil you can't eat because of him. Even the smell of it.) To add on an apartment. (He got to keep the house through a conspiracy inspired by his mother.)

Then he realized what he didn't want. To be married anymore. To you. And now he's with Rayleen, an airhead.

The idea is to look good, you tell the stylist. That's the idea.

Things the stylists insist upon: a fireplace, a cappuccino maker. Toronto once a year, loyalty, techno music. A stuffed toy.

What's going on out there?

Suzanne: Still snowing.

The streets have become impossibly narrow. Snowbanks muscling the cars like ululating throats. The stylists win dance contests. Drink B52s, martinis.

You are here to learn how to become vulnerable again. How to give yourself over. They like a nice glass, fruit. They like their drinks to be blue, orange slices; they tip flamboyantly. There's a big, decaying city in their past. Havana, maybe. Venice. They have no past.

The stylist absolutely insists upon silence at certain hours. Watching the February snow make the sky listless, the slob ice on the harbour lifting in swells so gentle it seems the couch moves beneath them. Hand-knit socks. Original art. Brand names: Le Château, Swatch, Paderno. To watch the dusk settle. Soap operas. The primacy of their cats.

Suzanne has one item in her fridge: dehydrated miniature crabs. She can see the whole city from her window in the Battery.

Your mother has been begging you for years to get your hair streaked. You have breakfast together and she puts down her fork.

Enough, your mother says. She leans over the table and touches your cheek with the back of her hand. You have been going with the salt over the eggs. You stop. And you go and go and go with the salt. Then you toss it across the kitchen.

You have made everything soft for him, like whipped cream.

There he is in the La-Z-Boy, hungover, misty-eyed.

I made a mistake, he says, I fucked someone.

Enough, you say.

Your mother cannot understand, nor will she accept, that you don't want streaks. You had no money in law school. Sometimes you were hungry. You left home, and your mother had to shovel. Sleeping pills. It got dark so early. There aren't even streetlights out that way. Her asthma. She'd have to walk through waist-deep snow and stop to use her inhaler. Icicles glinting. Leaks in the roof. You hear her smoke over the phone. A pause while she smokes. You hear the whir of the microwave, the bell. You hear the ice in her glass of scotch. You hear the icicles dripping outside. You hear her crying. What will make you stop crying, Mom?

She says, Have you thought about streaks?

Your husband wants to be an actor. He wants to give up his career as a bank manager. He wants a break from the kids. He wants the kids in his arms. He wants to go bankrupt, be a filmmaker. He has begun to identify with the clients whose assets he's been forced to seize. They aren't such bad guys.

The stylist takes a pair of scissors from the jar of blue liquid. Snaps them twice, flicking drops.

Suzanne's hair is short, stucco-like in texture, blond with ironic roots. Black-framed glasses. The bones of her hips pressing the red plastic jeans. Her shirt is clingy, reveals her belly button, a piercing. There are two kinds of hair, you've been told. The long and wispy: fuck-me hair. The short and androgynous: fuck-you hair.

You don't have the money now nor you will ever have the money to get your hair done every four months, which is how often you must in order to keep the roots from showing. You do not like roots. You hate them. You will not incur the extra expense just now when your bastard prick of a husband, who has run up every jointly owned credit card, who has spent the nest egg saved to help your mother retire early and not have to wade through snowbanks with her inhaler. The bastard prick has a spending disorder, in fact, hitherto unmentioned, and has left you with half his debt, which is the law, and is seeing an air-head, and you can't trust him to come up his half of the. You won't incur the extra expense for anything because you had to buy a new house and a second-hand car, the engine of which is tied together with dental floss.

Suzanne says, You're thinking colour.

Yes I am.

You need colour.

Yes I do.

I'm thinking streaks.

So am I.

When you are in your ninth month with Adrian, a youth hurls his chair across the courtroom at you. You see one metal leg blur past your temple. You've prosecuted this kid several times. Perhaps five. His sister also. Almost all the girls who appear in youth court are named Amanda. They are named after Rachel's daughter on the discontinued soap opera *Another World*. Most of the boys are named Cory. The boy leaps onto a table and is striding across the backs of the fixed seating. The judge has a button on his desk for moments like these. He presses the button, his black robes puff with air, and the safety door clicks quietly closed behind him. You can see him in the small square window of the door peering out to watch the action.

You think: Judge Burke has saved himself. You are taken up with a giddiness. Judge Burke strikes you as humorously prissy. You are trembling with a fit of suppressed giggles. But as the boy gets closer, your initial feeling about Judge Burke changes. You realize his decision to save himself and leave you, along with the handful of spectators, three security guards, three more youth also scheduled to appear before him this morning — Judge Burke's decision is a sound one. Certain men, given the appropriate circumstances, will behave with decisive and thorough self-centredness that smacks of sound judgement. Burke is elderly, completely unable to defend himself against a physical attack. Batty, even. His pronouncements are usually unsound. You often have to say, Judge Burke, I can see you're angry because your face is getting red, and I can tell by the tone of your voice that you are upset because you are speaking very loudly, but I feel I have to continue. You say things like this for the benefit of the court stenographer so the records will reflect Judge Burke's demeanour, should he come to the batty conclusion that he should charge you with contempt. Right now Judge Burke is nowhere to be seen. Right now a young man named Cory is going to kill you just before you give birth to your son, Adrian. As far as you know there have never been any Adrians on *Another World*. The youth is leaping, you have a contraction that doubles you, the security guards have him, water pours down your legs.

The male stylists are openly gay, mavericks, blithe, built. But it's the women who interest you. The women are beautiful, or look beautiful, stubbornly independent, current, childless. They enter and win lip-sync and wet T-shirt contests. At home in airports. Their families make allowances. They don't shovel. At Christmas they are the most extravagant, most deflated by the aftermath of unwrapped presents. They are the babies in the family. They're allowed to pick at the turkey. Suzanne brings you to the porcelain sink with the scoop for the neck. You lean back, close your eyes. You are determined to enjoy this.

She says, You don't have to hold your neck like that.

You have been holding your neck. You let your neck go loose. You are submitting. You let go. The salon falls away. Your scalp is a grass fire. You would kiss something if you could, or drift to sleep. The long, greying hair is such a weight. The hose makes you tingle all over. A hot, delicate raking. She's raking you to the surface of yourself. She drops the hose. Squirts a thread of viscous cherry over your scalp and begins with her fingers. She lets her nails graze. No one has touched you like this since your husband left. You almost kiss the snow white inside of Suzanne's wrist.

You are alone. It's your husband's night with the kids. Since your husband left, you have been falling asleep early in the evening. You haven't bought a TV. You got to keep the CD player but you only have a handful of CDs. You have listened to Cat Stevens's *Greatest Hits* so often you can. At first you kept the radio on all the time. A cheap radio in every room. Then you got tired of the radio. You listen hard but there's nothing to hear. A row of icicles falls from the eaves startling you so badly

you almost. You don't turn on the lights. You see your neighbour across the street pull into his driveway, his headlights
lighting up falling snow. He can't see you in your window
because the lights are off. He has asked you over for a glass of
wine. Once you awoke to the sound of him shovelling your
driveway. He gets out of the car and the light over his porch
comes on. He looks up into the sky. He's standing in his driveway with his hands in his pockets, his head tilted back. He stays
that way. Your fridge cuts in. Nothing moves on the street for a
long time, no cars, just the snow. Your neighbour goes inside
and you are alone. You are very much alone.

Suzanne fits a rubber skullcap over your head. The skullcap is
full of holes and she tugs strands of hair through each hole
with a metal hook. It hurts so much you think you might cry.
Then you do cry. Suzanne doesn't make a big deal of it. She's
seen all this before. She keeps pulling your hair.

That's the price, she says. She paints your hair with a foaming chemical. It's an awful stink, poisonous and angry. It makes
you feel exuberant.

Everyone has left the Aquarena because of the storm and your
mother hasn't come. Your coach switches off all the lights.
They make a thwack noise when they go off, and the fila-
ments burn pink then blue. The pool is empty and has gone
still. The pool is a chameleon and it has changed its skin so it
resembles nothing more than a swimming pool. It has become
invisible. Your thirteenth birthday is coming and very soon

you will lose interest in diving. One day you can think of nothing else, you are haunted. The next day diving hardly exists. You can't remember anything about it. You let your mother sleep in.

The storm has closed roads. Where is your mother? Your coach drives you home. The Trans Am flies through white-outs. You lose the road. The flame on the hood swallowed by the mouth. You have been saying. Talking. Telling him. Your eyes two soft plums, and a soft plum in your throat. Your heart is aching, but your heart is your eyes and you have two and they are bruised and weeping. Your coach pulls over. You pull over into Lovers Lane together. The trees slap the windows, paw the roof. He cups his hand under your chin and he kisses you. He gently sucks a bright plum from your throat. He kisses and kisses. You have never. Nothing will ever be as wonderful as this. You give yourself over/over/over.

You want Suzanne to give you some advice before you leave, and she does. She tells you that from now on you must use a round brush. She holds a mirror behind so you can see how sharp the cut is. You can see your neck. You don't recognize yourself from this angle. She's sprayed you and blown the whole thing dry so your hair feels as hard as a helmet. The blond is called ash and it glints like a tough metal.

Grace

On the shiny collar of her black tuxedo jacket, at a potluck after the wedding, Eleanor notices a ladybug. Orange shell, two black spots. Under the jacket she wears a crimson dress. The skirt a pattern of folded, satin diamonds, each diamond held with a red bead, so that if she were to attain grace, or spill her beer, or be overwhelmed with some fleeting infatuation — she shouldn't drink in the afternoon; she can see herself in Glenn Marshall's sunglasses, her black patent leather purse like a match head folded in the flame of her skirt — if she were visited by a moment of grace, the beads of the dress might drop to the grass and the diamonds unfold into butterflies. She grips the wet beer bottle. Too cold to be outside. The tulle under her skirt scratchy against her bare legs. She'll shave them before the reception. Where is Philip? At the heart of every-thing, she thinks, is the question of behaving with grace. He is falling in love with someone else. They have an understanding, is the phrase people say. Couples who agree to open marriages, an understanding.

A big wind lifts the umbrella out of the hole in the centre of the plastic table and it pirouettes for a few seconds across the lawn on its white metal spike. Glenn Marshall makes a swipe for it, arm raised, fist empty. What she has decided: She will sleep with Glenn Marshall. An understanding is something for which you must acquire a taste, like all the other great things in life: coffee, wine, oysters, bungee jumping. A crowd of guests move out of the path of the careening umbrella. It knocks against the picket fence. A paper napkin flutters off the table and dips, like a dove shot out of the sky, a gash of lipstick on its breast. The crystal bowl of strawberries catches the sun, a tiny prism shoots across its sharp rim. The rowing shells on Quidi Vidi Lake glide fast. A team of women with yellow caps hold the oars above the water. They lean forward, they lean back. A riot of sparkles bursts around the prow. The last rower raises her hand to her cheek and is obliterated in the glare.

The ladybug on Eleanor's jacket is still anchored. She's here somewhere, this woman Philip's seeing.

Eleanor closes her eyes. The afternoon sways, the lawn, the voices. The summer is almost over. She can smell fall. Once at the Ship Inn Glenn Marshall put his hand on the small of her back. She'd been dancing in a black minidress and the cotton was damp.

He said, What are you doing?

Getting a beer. What are you doing?

It's dangerous, talking to you.

Dangerous?

You have beautiful legs.

That was last summer, the same hint of fall. Just that, his hand on her back, the cotton damp with sweat. *You have beautiful legs.* She was ahead of him, leaning into the crowded bar, one heel lifting out of her shoe. He steadied her.

She can see Philip in the sunroom window, listening to a woman with a blond ponytail. This must be the woman. She's on tiptoe, he bends his ear toward her. Eleanor sees him yank his tie. Her mouth close to Philip's ear. Then a cloud moves, making the window darken, and she can't see him.

What's Philip doing, she asks Glenn Marshall.

Philip is having a good time. Believe me.

She feels the earth turning. The heels of her sandals driven into mud beneath the wet grass. She'd made a rice salad with sesame oil, red peppers. Last night the taxi driver said, See that moon, that's weather. I had a wife once who could make a meal out of nothing. You had your moose, you had your garden. I got a different wife now, different altogether.

Eleanor was making everyone tell the moment they had come closest to death.

I like moments, she says, any kind of moment. Cut to the climax.

Glenn Marshall was once in a helicopter, sighting the neck of a galloping moose with a tranquilizing rifle, and they came near a cliff, and whatever happened with the wind, the helicopter dropped for ten seconds. He told the story while buttering a roll. Turning the knife over and over to clean both sides in the bread. He said in accidents like this, the blades keep turning, driving down like a corkscrew, decapitating passengers.

Eleanor told about the crashing Nepalese tour bus, the front wheel over the cliff edge, the TVs bolted to the ceiling still blaring some Indian musical with a harem of dancers poised on three tiers of a fountain, all sawing on miniature violins. Big breasts, pillowy hips. When the second wheel of the bus thumped over the edge of the cliff, the fountain hung sideways, the dancers still perched, still grinning and sawing away on the violins in jubilant Technicolor, defying gravity. She had seen, through the window at her shoulder, fire smeared over the steel side. They were on fire. She and Sadie sleeping under a single bedsheet. The windshield shattered and fell into their laps. The bluish glass tumbling into the folds of the sheet, caught in their hair. They had raised their arms to cover their faces.

And there they were, in Nepal. What opulence, how quiet. The pressing crowd squished them, lifted them off their feet. They were borne out of the bus and fell on their knees and got up quick, quick.

Get away from the bus, get away before it blows.

Dawn; a woman in a sari on a dusty road with a water jug on her head and the sun coming up behind her. The real moment is the flutter of the sari. The snap and thwonk of fabric in the breeze. The silence. Someone taking out a map that crackled in the hot air like eggshells. But Eleanor stops telling the story just as the second wheel of the bus flops over the cliff.

Leave your audience hanging.

She says, Beneath you could see buses that had already crashed, crumpled on the rocks. Then the second wheel rolled over the edge and we could feel the bus rocking.

Glenn leaned back and rested his arm over her chair. She could smell the muggy, spring-like sweat of his body. The nearness of his arm made her blush.

She thought: And Philip wants to leave me.

These were the categories of moments: the most famous person they'd ever met, the most romantic moment ever experienced, the most embarrassing. Earliest memory. Luckiest moment. The last time you peed your pants.

Constance told about waking in a field when she was seven with a bull eating grass, snorting water droplets on her cheek, horns yellowed like an old toilet. How she ran, hot pee trickling down her legs, yellow on her white ankle socks. When she'd climbed the fence, stopped to catch her breath, leaned over to puke, she could see the blue sky and clouds in the shiny black patent leather shoes an aunt had sent from St. John's. She lights a cigarette and blows the wedding veil out of her face.

She says, Will someone get me out of this contraption?

Constance grew up around the bay, an only child, raised by her grandmother. She says she was bathed in the kitchen in a big galvanized tub in front of a wood stove. Can this be true?

She remembers when television arrived in Newfoundland. They all gathered in one house to watch. She's a chef with a Master's in Religious Studies. Medieval witches. Magic, black and white. Eleanor has watched Constance paint braided pastry with melted butter, skin rabbits, flick dollops of fresh cream off a wooden spoon into chocolate mousse.

Once Philip had made Eleanor open her mouth and close her eyes. He'd had candles, they'd smoked some dope, him scrabbling under the bed. *Keep 'em closed.* A ball bearing dinging back and forth in the metal can he shook, *I said keep 'em closed,* and the raucous sputtering, her mouth blocked with Reddi Wip. Loops of Reddi Wip over her nipples, her chin, her nose, her hair.

Constance looks like cotton candy in the dress. Eleanor can't, for the moment, imagine her in other clothes. She was made for the wedding dress. Busty and pink-cheeked. Satin is perfect for her, iceberg cool and pleasure affirming. She was made, actually, to be in a Russian novel; a kitchen with a fireplace as big as a bed, the gamekeeper banging on the door with a wooden staff, a brace of quail over his shoulder, and there is Constance presiding over blood puddings, her four children in muslin walking in the pink cherry orchard.

The whole wedding dress swishes from side to side as she hands out puff pastry with brie and caramelized onions. Her auburn curls sliding from the combs. The low scooped neck. She'd pulled the whole wedding off by herself without complaint. She had enjoyed it. Constance knows how to get by on nothing, she and Ted, the four children, and the scabrous, moulting husky with an eye infection — they are always broke. But when it comes to a party, Constance is easily extravagant. What's money for? A tiny glass tube of saffron she'd picked up at a specialty store on the way back from the Sally Ann where she'd bought the girls' jeans.

Yesterday Eleanor had visited and Constance was sitting at the kitchen table, smoking (an orange silk blouse, that's the sort of thing she wears), cheek resting on her hand and the counter full of loaves of bread, the tops glistening with butter. More dough rising. She sat in front of the window, taking a break. Making Eleanor a cup of tea. The rowing shells on the lake passing by her shoulder. Yesterday the lake was still, and the oars touched down and came up splashless. The kittens knocking over the jade plant. Giant piles of laundry. A stack of books about the plague, one on alchemy. She'd had four children, each a year apart. Alchemy she knew; the Pill she didn't bother with.

Eleanor had said, How do you do it? The bread. Constance waved a dismissive hand in the direction of the counter.

The bread makes itself, she'd said. There's nothing to bread. But the lamb. She opened a magazine and tossed it toward Eleanor so she could read the recipe.

Maybe if I'd learned to cook, Eleanor said vaguely, snapping the pages of the magazine. She stopped at a perfume ad, a crystal decanter stopper trailing down a woman's throat, her pouty lips parted.

Or wore perfume.

Constance narrowed her eyes, then opened them wide, tapped her cigarette vigorously.

You have to behave with grace, is my advice, Constance said.

Grace is boring.

Nevertheless.

You could uninvite her, Eleanor said.

I wouldn't give her the satisfaction.

And now Constance is married to Ted. The service held on Signal Hill, the wind whipping her veil into a beehive over her head until the bridesmaid caught it and batted it into submission. The priest is the man who shot the windows out of that church you can see from the highway. Red paint along the white clapboard, "These Windows Shot Out By A Catholic Priest."

Eleanor opens her purse, drops her corsage inside, and snaps it closed. She lifts the neck of her jacket. The ladybug is gone. She'd wanted to show her daughter, Gabrielle. They'd been looking for a ladybug months ago, to make a wish.

Frank Harvey is talking. Frank says he found himself doing the husband thing. A stone fireplace in the basement, some plumbing, other couples on Friday night talking about this shade of wallpaper or upgrading gas barbeques, and all the while he hated himself.

You discover that you are an asshole, he says. He winces. Tilts the lemon slice in his gin from side to side.

An asshole, he says. That's what happened to me. It was a terrible thing. I took up yoga.

The moment you faced your worst fear, says Eleanor.

She tells about her mother trapped in her living room with a white weasel or mink. After Eleanor's father died. Eleanor had been seventeen, in Stephenville, wrapped in a snowstorm, a giant wooden custard cone banging off the side of an abandoned convenience store. She's trying to work it into the screenplay she's writing — the custard cone squeaking on its hinges. Ice in her eyelashes. Later, in the student residence, the phone ringing down the hall, running to catch it, and it's her mother, in her kitchen in St. John's, standing on the counter. Somehow a rodent, fat as her thigh, long as her arm, had gotten into her house.

A white weasel or mink tearing through the green and gold shag carpeting, crazed. Eleanor could hear its piping squeals. Her mother, a tall woman, neck bent awkwardly, the back of her head touching the stuccoed ceiling. The stucco swirled with a scrub brush, a new idea then. They had a spiral staircase, a smoky mirrored fireplace. They had an open-concept upstairs, a lake, and in the winter veils of snow sashayed all over the dark ice. The snow could come up to her mother's waist, and Howard, a mentally handicapped man who lived down the road, would come and shovel. Eleanor's mother would bring him a Pepsi with ice, which he paused long enough to drink, his frosty breath hanging, his fluorescent orange cap. Just the two of them with no one around for miles. Her mother standing beside him, waiting for the glass.

And this became her mother's life after her father died; she was only occasionally terrified; the mink's eye flashing that alien green of trapped animals and then black again, under the dining-room table.

Most erotic moment without touching. The cork of a wine bottle rolling over a faded yellow rose on the tablecloth under Glenn Marshall's palm. His hand on her back. That might have been a moment of grace. The Ship Inn on a summer night blocked with people, standing space only, some event at the Hall getting out, the band deafening, summer dresses, tanned faces. The way the light slowly tinted the sky over the South Side Hills indigo, yellowish, pale blue. The desire to keep going, another bar, someone's house, her new sandal destroyed. The sidewalk on Duckworth Street. A police cruiser slowing beside them and moving on. Glenn Marshall had whispered something in her ear, I'd like to go home with you. She had sobered up immediately. The cool breeze coming up from the harbour. The smell of the sea.

I'd like to do nice things to you, he'd said. How illicit and tender it had sounded. Sweetly wrong. Hokey and forward! The prim fervour with which she explained she could never, ever, ever hurt her husband.

Frank Harvey is still talking about the moment you discover you're an asshole. A Sunday afternoon in Bannerman Park, he says, hungover, fragile, children making the diving board reverberate, wind in the leaves, and it hit me. It was so cleansing, such a relief. He's smiling at everyone. Frank Harvey is holding court. The sun hits his balding forehead. It gleams as if he is physically projecting his new wisdom. He's good to have at a wedding; he's the entertainment.

Eleanor thinks: How dangerous to fall in love with Frank Harvey. She could always do that if Philip leaves. It would be *torrid*. Yes, there would be battles in public, dishes shattered, lovemaking outdoors, in movie theatres, planes. Bike trips across Canada, leanness, bracing, voluntary poverty. She would have to shave her head or become vegetarian. Type on a manual typewriter. Maybe take up smoking. She could be a female Ernest Hemingway, grow a beard. It would be invigorating. Philip, stunned, shaking his head at some luncheon. Philip regretting his blonde. But Eleanor is already too old for Frank. His lovers are all under twenty-five, they are giggly, svelte, and have asymmetrical haircuts. Eleanor doesn't have a haircut.

You see what I mean, says Frank Harvey, you're an asshole, you have somewhere to go from there, don't you? I rejoiced. No, seriously, I did. It was so unequivocal — my assholeness. The clouds broke and the sun poured down, cleansing me. I was cleansed.

Frank takes a moment to close his eyes and lift his palms and handsome face to whatever power cleansed him. This is ninety-two percent delivery, but the content he means. He means what he says. Timing, he understands. He's parodying himself parodying himself. He's dead serious. He opens his eyes and says almost viciously, I was brand spanking new.

Is Frank Harvey what they mean when they say bipolar? Or is he truly very, very near enlightenment? What enlightenment looks like: his eyes are so clear. He is so bursting with health. So goddamn sexy. Eleanor decides enlightenment would take too much energy. A lot of honesty. She's hardly ever deceitful — she imagines herself hacking a path of truth through a vast field with a machete, stopping only briefly to wipe the sweat from her brow.

But Philip believes he is duty-bound to lie whenever it makes life easier. Eleanor imagines herself from an aerial view, the path she's hacked winding in on itself, a spiral. Then she briefly allows herself to imagine Frank Harvey's penis. The word *dong* leaps to mind. Something big and friendly. The sound of cymbals at the gateway of the Forbidden City. The whack of a baseball against a bat. Ying yang, ding dong. With Frank she could be oblique, like a heroine in a bodice ripper, Frank, *take* me.

The smell of cinnamon from a tray Constance passes under her nose and Eleanor is back in India with Sadie, ten, no twelve years ago. Icy air-conditioning, thwack of ceiling fans. How real it becomes for her sometimes. She can smell it. They were asked to be extras in a movie. Two shady-looking men outside the Salvation Army hostel in Bombay. They said, Meet us here at five in the morning. We'll fly you to Bangor. You'll be paid. Eleanor terrified, Sadie gung-ho.

Is this a good idea?

Sadie: Are you kidding? This is the *movies*.

With yoga, says Frank Harvey, there is so much pain. I tried to bury my self-hatred in pain. The instructor was so good. She really hurt me.

The Indian movie agents came for Sadie and Eleanor at five a.m. Drove them to the outskirts of the city, and beyond, into a dry landscape, almost desert. How had Sadie become so brave? And somehow this drive, during which Eleanor believed her twenty-three-year-old life was ending, and during which Sadie sang Joni Mitchell songs for the two men who had abducted them, her elbows flung over the front seat — *he bought her a dishwasher and a coffee percolator* — singing with deep feeling, though they are too young to understand how sad or practical a dishwasher can be — all of this becomes vividly present. She remembers even the crack in the window, the rubber Ganesh (why is he blue) jumping on an elastic hanging from the rearview mirror. She was once this: a woman in the back of a car in the desert about to be killed/be in a Bollywood movie.

And now she is what? Philip *might* be leaving. How will she support herself and Gabrielle? She has to finish her screenplay. She could get at least three or four thousand in development money if she tried. Even if the film went nowhere, four thousand. There are avenues. A little low-budget video thingy. A seventeen-year-old girl in Stephenville going to art school, old army barracks buried in snow, the El Dorado Lounge, the Grim Reaper, losing her virginity, her father's death.

The most erotic moment without touching: watching the nineteen-year-old boy, the first guy she'd ever slept with, sculpting a clay torso. Squeezing water from a sponge over the breasts, making the clay shiny like licked chocolate, a drip hanging on the nipple, the slosh while he dips the sponge, the water hitting the clay with a patter; he talks to her while his muddy hands smooth the muscles in the torso's belly, the ribs, the clavicle. He sponges the curve of the torso's neck, and Eleanor's hand creeps up by itself to her own neck, and they both notice and laugh. They laugh, but she is blushing, hot.

The screenplay was taking forever. The penultimate scene, a Halloween party in a sprawling bar. That much would be cheap enough to shoot. Sometimes she still thinks about feasibility. She used to think about it always. But the more true the script becomes — the closer she is to describing the loss she felt with her father's death — the less she cares if it's feasible. Sandra, the lead, is drunk in the penultimate scene. She has made up her mind to lose her virginity. The town is buried in snowdrifts; it's a white film. White. Oh, the young girl Eleanor imagines playing the lead. Beautiful because she's that strange mix of child and adult, a changeling, like all sixteen-year-olds, but ordinary-looking too. The camera will always be close up on her face. The boy Sandra has decided to sleep with, a student at the school, is dressed as the Grim Reaper. He goes to the bar for beer and another Grim Reaper comes to her table and takes her by the wrist.

Eleanor looks for Sadie, who is supposed to be at this wedding party but who is late. Always late. She's in picture-lock, the message on the answering machine said. The film she's working on; they've got the final edit. She won't miss the potluck, she promises. I'll be there, okay. She's bringing Peach Melba isn't she? How could she miss the potluck? But it's almost over already, the potluck, and there is no Sadie.

She and Sadie were not killed in the desert by talent scouts as Eleanor had thought they would be! Instead they were extras in a Bollywood movie. They met a harem of dancers. Women who had been trained in the art of classical Indian dancing since they were five years old. Women who wore pale pancake makeup to lighten their dark skin. Kohl around their eyes. Plump, luscious women who fell asleep on wooden benches at one o'clock in the afternoon, dressed in brown calico house-coats. The Vamp (in the dance number, she peeks coyly out from behind a palm tree, searching for the Prince she's about to seduce away from his virtuous wife) had chased Sadie around the change room. Sadie letting out yelps, leaping over benches, the Vamp trying to pinch her bum, the other dancers squealing, shrieking. Sadie backing her bum into a corner, bent double with giggles. Moments later the dancers huddled together, whispering, and they turned as a group. What, Sadie demanded. The Vamp stepped forward: You both must shave your under-arms, it's terrible. To appear on film like that. Have you no shame?

There had been a poolside scene; a long line of dancers held striped beach balls over their heads and then fell sideways into the water, one after the other, like dominoes. Sadie and Eleanor among them, arms raised over their heads. Gloriously hairy armpits. They stood in line, the smell of chlorine and the burning sun, the music bursting into action, the Vamp shimmy-ing to the water's edge, tossing her gorgeous black hair, slitting her sexy eyes at the camera, and one by one, the dancers fell into the water. None of them could swim. They began to drown as soon as they hit the water, the revved-up, hysterical music droning to silence, long black hair floating on the water, choking, coughing, panic. The cameramen reaching over the edge of the pool with poles. Sadie and Eleanor dragging the young women to the side, saving their lives after each take.

Eleanor walks across the lawn toward the house. She hears Dawn Clark's voice above everyone else: I *know* the Net. You've got a demographic of nineteen-year-old males, what are you going to do, sell them walking canes? I don't *think* so.

Eleanor goes inside, gets herself another beer from the fridge. She thinks, This beer will be the ruin of me. But it's cold; the frost smoking off the lip of the bottle cheers her up. There is Philip. She walks over to him and lays her hand on his neck. He turns and looks at her, smiling while he talks. He has forgotten, for the moment, that he wants to leave her. Whatever he is telling Constance is more important. Eleanor and Philip are together at the potluck. They might go on forever. They are surrounded by friends. The rowers glide past on the lake. The room is full of flowers. The children are playing in their fancy clothes. Gabrielle waves to her from the lawn, the long grass combing her lemon dress.

Philip telling Constance about his book. Constance holding her forehead in her hand, elbow on the table. She taps a cigarette. She's listening to globalization, still in the wedding dress.

The Swedes moving traffic from the left to the right side of the road, Philip says, without a hitch, overnight. Things can change overnight.

Eleanor has an overwhelming urge to pour her beer down the back of Philip's shirt. How dare he think of abandoning her. She has given up travelling the world with Sadie for him. They had promised to travel all their lives together, she and Sadie, no matter what. She has given up jungles, and rides in rubber dinghies in murky lagoons, and pyramids. Why had she ever given up being who she was to love Philip? (He knows everything, everything, and is handsome, his big hands on the cheeks of her bum, last week she came in from a rain that bounced like ball bearings on the pavement, the house booming with Glenn Gould, so loud it was tactile, in the banister, in the linoleum, the Goldberg Variations, she yelled his name, and waited, and yelled again, but he couldn't hear over the music and the shower and the rain and up the stairs two at a time, her coat, a boot, her sock, her shirt, the jeans — dropping them as she went — the other boot, the sock, the underwear, the bra, and she stood on the other side of the shower curtain, waiting, listening, the bathroom foggy and hot and the leaves of the spider plant on the windowsill trembling from the music, she got in silently, he was standing with his eyes closed, his hands resting on his chest and she cupped his balls and his eyes flew open and he screamed. He scared her so much she screamed, and they stood as if electrified, her hand on his balls, screaming into each other's face, then laughing, then fucking, the wet slap of their bodies.) He thinks it's wrong to stay in a relationship if you are in love with someone else. He does not believe in *weathering through*, or *for the children*, or *because you promised*. He believes, simply, in doing what you want.

First of all, Philip doesn't believe in anything. He believes strongly in not believing in anything. He believes Eleanor's whole problem is that she wants so desperately for there to be a *right* way. She has been too chicken-shit to shed this last vestige of her Catholic upbringing: the desire for a universal moral code, which, once understood, leaves only the small matter of putting it into practice. If he were to believe in something, it would be: admit what you want; get what you want. This line of action requires great stores of bravery. Apparently it's not as easy as it sounds. But to do otherwise, Philip believes, sets in motion a whole chain of actions and events which totally fucks up not only your life but everyone's life with whom you come in contact. To do otherwise is to act dishonestly.

There is something so blazing and committed about this baldly self-centred stand that Eleanor loves him all the more for it. She refuses to love him less. He's stuck with her. He is what she wants.

Eleanor goes back out on the lawn. Glenn Marshall is where she left him. She'll tell Glenn Marshall about the Taj Mahal, the warm marble and smell of feet. They'd seen a man levitate in front of the Taj Mahal.

But Glenn loves Newfoundland. He doesn't like heat, prefers cool weather. He wouldn't want to be on top of the Pink Palace with lithe monkeys. She has told him before, she suddenly remembers. She has told him that story before, about the

Bollywood movie. Glenn Marshall had been mildly interested. He had listened, but he shook his head and said he'd never go there. Why would he? He loves Newfoundland. As if there were just the two choices: the Taj or Little Island Cove. He loves being in the woods by himself, he has a cabin, can build a lean-to, set snares; he does some ice fishing, he likes the quiet.

Who is she kidding, she could never love Glenn Marshall. But if she slept with him. Maybe if she slept with him. Things can change overnight. The entire city of Stockholm, was it? Driving on the other side of the road as though they always had.

Frank Harvey says, And I had an epiphany, alone in Bannerman Park on a Sunday afternoon. I realized it was *okay* to be an ass-hole. I rushed out to tell my wife about the affairs I'd had, you see, I had already forgiven myself.

What was Glenn Marshall's most erotic moment without touching? Eleanor can only think of the galloping moose. He had kissed her on New Year's Eve and said, How do you like a moustache?

Ted says, Constance sent me flowers in the middle of a rain-storm — someone announced it over the intercom at the bookstore. I was in the back room tearing off the covers of old Harlequin romances. A big box of white roses.

Ivory, says Constance.

The salesgirls falling all over themselves to find a card, says Ted.

The first night Eleanor slept at Philip's apartment; walking up the steep hill from Kibitzer's, broken beer bottles glittering by the curbs, someone's white bedsheets flapping on a line. She walked under the sheets, the damp cotton stiff with frost when it brushed over her face. She turned to watch him, a big hand bashing through, the clothespins pinging into the air, and then the rest of him tumbling, falling. They were twenty-one and he had a three-year-old daughter. A light came on in the row of public housing, then another. They were rolling down the hill in the sheet. Grass, mud, stones, sky, stars. The sheet wrapped around them like a cocoon they wriggled out of together.

A snowy afternoon at four o'clock; walking past the war memorial with his three-year-old child on her shoulders, Eleanor counting change for a block of cheese. They had the macaroni already. They were a family overnight, some sort of family. The change in her hand just enough! The child's shiny red boots hanging beneath her chin. Dusk swooping down on Duckworth Street, the second-hand bookstore still lit. Slush seeping into her boots. Holding tight to the child's ankles. Later, the steam rising from the pot in the kitchen, she and the child painted fish on the clear plastic shower curtain. The who-she-was disappearing fast, gobbled by the who-she-is.

Frank Harvey says his wife went insane with jealousy when he told her about the affairs.

I've avoided women like that ever since, jealous women. I can smell it, and if I get even the faintest whiff, I'm gone a hundred miles in the other direction.

He sounds so right, Eleanor thinks. She vaguely understands that everything Frank Harvey says is informed by the year of silence he spent in a monastery in Korea. Frank Harvey, the mime, had not spoken for an entire year of his life. It helped, he'd said, that no one spoke English. Cut down on the desire to blurt, he'd said. You come to understand the sublime beauty of chitchat, the fragmentary, absurd, chaotic, feral meaninglessness of everything we say. Whatever else about Frank Harvey, he is a talented mime. He can do the glass wall thing, of course, and the Michael Jackson moonwalk, but he can also run on the spot in slow motion as if he were being chased in a nightmare, his bones melting, and then he is caught and devoured by some unnameable monster you can almost smell. He can hold invisible animals in his hands, quelling their struggles for escape. She loves how convincing Frank Harvey is. Convincing is the thing to be, Eleanor decides; it doesn't matter what you're convincing about.

I came to love talk, Frank Harvey says, I live for it. And I learned how to tell a joke, he says. You must never telegraph the laugh. Let the material do the work. The best joke I ever told, I waited a year to deliver the punch line.

What was the joke, Tiffany White asks. Tiffany is a bright, new nurse who has arrived from Thunder Bay. Eleanor realizes she is taking Frank seriously.

That was the joke, says Frank Harvey. You didn't get it?

What was?

The joke was it took a year to tell the joke.

Frank turns back to Eleanor. We parted after that, he says, speaking of his wife. There was nothing left to salvage.

It's some Buddhist idea of Frank's, Eleanor thinks, we can't possess each other. We shouldn't even want to. She has an ache in her chest as if she had been Frank Harvey's wife, the one he had cheated on a thousand million times. She wants to defend herself against his airtight argument, that jealousy is vile. What kind of man doesn't talk for a year?

Constance takes a tray of honey garlic meatballs from the oven. The woman with the blond ponytail is sitting next to Philip. Amelia Kerby from British Columbia doing a PhD on Canadian ecofeminist novels. A gold lamé dress: she had met Leonard Cohen in Greece, had somehow gotten invited into his limousine as it pulled away from a concert. Fans tearing open their blouses and squashing their breasts against the car windows as they pulled out of the garage.

She says, I put my hand on his crotch, he was wearing black leather pants, and the sun through the window made the leather hot. I couldn't help myself.

Eleanor: Your hand on his crotch, that's not without touching. It's supposed to be an erotic moment without touching.

The first night she and Philip slept together, he was sitting in an armchair and she sat on the frayed arm, in a homey downtown bar. *The Last Tango in Paris* was playing on a snowy screen bolted above the bar. Brando with the butter. Maria Schneider, those breasts. Empty apartment. The French are forever living in empty rooms with high ceilings and open windows, curtains.

Sadie's boyfriend, Maurice, has such an apartment. He wanders around it all day with a glass of something, and sighs, and writes something down, and wanders around the apartment some more. For this he gets a fair bit of money. As far as Eleanor can tell, that's all he does, but Eleanor doesn't speak French, so. Schneider's heels clattering on the tiles, the butter. The last movie ever about pleasure, expansive, extravagant, expensive, anger-incited, dangerous pleasure. Or pain. She isn't sure now.

At night in a hotel in Southern India, Bangor, monsoon rains drilling rivets in the corrugated tin roof, a week after the movie shoot; Sadie shook her awake. Sadie had opened her diary to an empty page. She was running her fingers through her hair and lice fell onto the clean paper. All those drowning dancers had lice.

We have them now, Sadie said.

Long shiny black ropes of hair floating in the aqua water, covering Eleanor's face and arms as she dragged the drowning dancers to the poolside after each shot.

You have them, said Eleanor. I don't have them.

The next day they were at a train station. Eleanor went to buy a drink and the train started to pull away without her. It was halfway out of the station gathering speed. Sadie's voice from a dark window, already in the white sun of the countryside, Jump on, jump on.

Eleanor ran and a soldier in khakis with a rifle leaned out of the last car and offered her his hand. He pulled her aboard, and she yelled into the countryside, rice fields flashing in the sun, I'm on the train, Sadie. Then she sat down on a sack of grain and hung her head, feeling her fast-beating heart and, at the nape of her neck, the crawling lice.

Eleanor opens her eyes and pulls the heel of her sandal slowly out of the mud. She has been out on the lawn most of the afternoon. She can feel the heat of a late summer sunburn. She turns, looks up at the bedroom window.

Constance and Ted have disappeared. And this is Ted's story, she thinks. His stepfather woke him with the tip of a kitchen knife pressing into his windpipe when he was fourteen. Ted inching his back up the wall, his palms squeaking against the floral wallpaper, until he's standing on tip-toe, the knife pressing hard into his throat. The most terrifying moment.

Ted says, My father died when I was three. After my stepfather arrived we weren't allowed in my mother's bedroom. That's why I let the children sleep with us whenever they want. They just pile in, all four of them and the dog. Constance can't stand it.

She hasn't seen Ted or Constance for an hour or more. They must be making love. Consummating the marriage. All the guests on the lawn filling their faces. The wedding dress on the hardwood floor, a sinking angel food cake.

Ted's brother Earl, a hulking rugby player, leans over the railing of the verandah, a champagne glass in his giant ginger-root hands, as delicate and incongruous as an icicle. Earl had gone to

New Brunswick with his wife after a bankruptcy; he had five children. He worked in a cola factory for a time and was electrocuted while moving an industrial appliance. Enough electricity to lift him off his feet, blow him across the floor, and smash him against the wall. The moment you came closest to death.

He says, I lived because I kept my eyes open. If I'd closed my eyes I would have completed the circuit, and self-combusted, and this is the truth of what happened, whether it's scientifically true or not.

When Earl recovered he bought himself a small wooden table where he could sit and write poetry. He wrote several poems every day and understood his interest to have been ignited by the bolt of electricity. He called Constance late at night and read her the poems long distance, and she boxed up all her Eliot and mailed it to him.

Eleanor has imagined, ever since she first heard the story, that the electrical bolt had blown through Earl, back into his past, powering the restaurant he ran, the jobs he gave all his friends, including Eleanor (who once dropped a bowl of cod chowder down the back of another waitress), reached all the way back to the moment when his stepfather held a knife to Ted's throat, and protected Ted in a web of blue crackly light. Because Earl, with his near seven-foot height and boulder chest, wasn't a talker. Ted did the philosophy degree; Chad, the youngest, roamed the country with his thumb, became a clothing designer; and Earl protected, just as he was doing now, leaning on the verandah, the glass tipped, his eyes squinted against the glare of the lake.

Eleanor says, What do you think grace is, Glenn?

She's thinking, if she could attain grace, even for a moment, everything would fall into place. The scenes of her film script would snap together like a Rubik's cube, the scales would fall from her husband's eyes, and he would recognize how lucky he was to have her; Frank Harvey would return to his wife, or at least call and tell her she had been right all along. All women would be right. Glenn is watching Earl too. He doesn't speak until Earl turns and walks through the screen door, holding his fingertips against the wood frame so it doesn't bang.

Below Constance's bedroom window, the sunroom window. She sees a white streak that might be Philip's shirt.

Weasels don't come in white, Glenn says.

The one in my mother's house was white. It might have been a mink. Like spilled milk. My mother stood on the kitchen counter and it ran through the rungs of the chairs under the dining-room table.

I don't believe it, he says.

But you believe Leonard Cohen and the squashed breasts? You believe Amelia Kerby?

Amelia, Eleanor overheard while getting her beer from the kitchen, has also made a smallish fortune designing aromatherapy atomizers to squirt (mist, was the verb Amelia used) in the faces of colicky babies to shut them up (encourage serenity, Amelia said). The gold lamé dress was shipped from Paris; it had been packed in helium.

What have you got in those atomizers, asked Constance. Agent Orange?

Amelia's uncle was a marine biologist. She had written a novel about eco-conscious cyborgs, a moral tale as yet unpublished because Amelia hasn't decided who to go with, apparently. She had bumped along the floor of the Atlantic in a two-person craft. There was nothing much to see down there, she said. It was dark.

Eleanor wants to tell Glenn Marshall she remembers him touching her back at the Ship Inn. Does he remember it? His hand on her back, a pulse of neon lighting up her bones, her hip, her ankle, all through. Once she heard Leonard Cohen dedicating a song to all the people who had conceived children listening to his music. The elegant arrogance of it. But Gabrielle was conceived that way. An attic bedroom in Toronto during a heat wave, a fitted bedsheet working its way off a coffee-coloured futon, she and Philip satiny with Toronto sweat. The whole day walking Yonge, crowds, bursts of music, exhaust, neon in daylight, sex shops with things she'd never seen before, battery-operated vaginas that could smoke a cigarette, the smell of hotdog stands. A food wrapper blew against her shin, squiggle of ketchup. Pastry shops. Even the breeze was hot. The sidewalk where they lived covered with blossoms. All part of their lovemaking, and Leonard Cohen singing about Joan of Arc. *Make your body cold, I'm going to give you mine to hold.*

They had a tiny fan jammed in the window that did nothing but make a noise that she felt on the edges of her teeth. This was the cement of her love for Philip: this attic room, the swelter of summer, Newfoundland a gazillion miles away. She went with him to write her first film script. She'd written a naked skydiver. Swinging like a lazy pendulum beneath the big red bulb of a parachute, the sky behind utterly blue.

She had dreamed a skydiver, and he compelled her to make him real. The room she and Philip shared was so small that when they both sat at their desks the backs of their chairs touched. He went to the university during the day, and when it started to get dark outside she would listen for his footsteps on the sidewalk under the window. Listen for his key, the sound of his knapsack hitting the floor, the zipper of his jacket, the Velcro of his sneakers, the cats rubbing against his legs. She anticipated him. Tried to piece together who he was, and he was this: the cracked leather of the knapsack, dusk, clammy heat, the sound of coffee beans being ground in the kitchen. The unrelenting desire to fuck. She promised herself all day she would wait for the little things, the kiss, to take his earlobe in her teeth, unbutton his shirt, take a long time between each button — but her desire leapt all over itself, and she would want him inside her, couldn't wait.

Glenn?

He might have fallen asleep. The children are throwing a Frisbee at the edge of the lake.

Eleanor says, I want to be full of grace. Then she's embarrassed. What is she talking about, at a wedding? She is clearly drunk. She firmly reminds herself: You can't be sexy and maudlin at the same time.

Glenn says, Grace is bestowed, you can't will it.

Grace is bestowed. Everything worth anything is like that, she thinks. You can't just know what you want and go get it, as Philip says. You wait. She closes her eyes. Watches the lake through her lashes. Wait for it to come to you. She can see the children, silhouettes, standing on the rim of the lake as if they will upend it. It's only late afternoon, there's still the evening, there's more drinking to do. There's a lot more drinking.

Frank Harvey says, It's about identity. My wife started to think of herself as us. What we made up together.

Frank is right. You have to be able to be alone. If only she could sleep with someone else. Once at the Ship Inn she could have gone home with Glenn Marshall. That first time with Philip she thought: I will spend the rest of my life with him. She thinks, I have never questioned this, and I have acted upon it. I have built a twisted organic life around the assumption that Philip was meant for me. She imagines the great coral reef around Australia as her life — as if Philip is Australia and she has accrued around the fact of him. Coral accrues.

But she's afraid to be alone. Gabrielle had been afraid last night too. What was it? Can she guess her father might be leaving them? (But he's not leaving Gabrielle, he has explained this patiently to Eleanor several times, she keeps forgetting. But you're leaving, aren't you? I might be leaving, yes. You might be. Yes, and Gabrielle will come with me half the time. Gabrielle will go with you? You're leaving and Gabrielle will go with you. Sure, she can be with me half the time. In some apartment. Yes. So it's me you're leaving. I might be leaving you, he says. And you think that will be good for Gabrielle? He shrugs. It won't be a good thing, he says, maybe a necessary thing. Gabrielle will be fine, he says. He turns back to the computer. He doesn't let one thing overlap with the other. He might be leaving, but right now he has to work on his book about globalization.)

Gabrielle sobbing at the foot of their bed, her upper lip shiny with mucous. Eleanor let Gabrielle drag her down the hall. They stood in the doorway, she and her seven-year-old daughter. Eleanor saw the streetlight hit the dull glass of the hobbyhorse's eye. She saw a rust-coloured flare thin as a needle in the button. Sinister and pulsing. Gabrielle terrified. It's alive. It's *thinking*. A horse's head on a stick. The wind blew hard against the house, the windowpane rattled, and the fierce light, deep in the horse's button eye, faded and went flat. Shadows of leaves tumbled over each other on the wall above the bed, like galloping hoofs, a spooked herd all turning at once. Gabrielle's hand sweaty in hers, her face wet, nose running.

Eleanor thinks, I'm such a *dupe*. The shame she feels is so overpowering she could throw up all the red wine she's been drinking, and the beer, and the goat cheese thingies. She could throw up over the red dress with its folds and beads. She decides she will go in there and kick Amelia Kerby and punch her, knock her teeth loose. I will cut her into pieces and wear a chunk of her around my neck on a rope until it rots. I will not speak to her, I will not notice her, I will be aloof, condescendingly kind, I will invite her to dinner parties, rise above it all, befriend her. I'll sleep with her myself.

Her skin gets cold, and she thinks just as suddenly, It's not so bad. I'll go to China. No one there will know Philip has left me. A clean, simple life in China. They'll never hear from her again. Someone had gone to China already, that doctor whose wife left him. There was a rumour he'd remarried, he was happy, had new children. Chinese children. The rowers have lined up next to the buoys. A team of women in orange tank tops. They just float while the coxswain harangues them. A shrill whistle. Eleanor thinks, it's very unlikely that I will go to China. Instead. Gradually, over time, I will get over Philip. My passion for Philip will cool. That's what happens. People *get over it*. They eventually get over it. This is the worst thing: to imagine normal without him.

Someone places her hands over Eleanor's eyes. Eleanor reaches up and touches the wrists. Sadie! Eleanor is so happy she feels sharp little tears.

You're here.

Did I miss anything?

Amelia Kerby. She's over there tossing back champagne.

The gall!

Gold lamé, the ponytail.

She looks short to me. Am I right?

Ecofeminist.

Hefty, I'm thinking.

Here on scholarship.

What's with the tinfoil dress? How Walmart.

You think?

Sure I think!

She's into aromatherapy.

Of course she is.

And bungee jumping.

He'll get tired real quick.

Naked, they bungee jump on the West Coast.

Real quick.

Eleanor hadn't taken the scene of the naked skydiver to the pitch meeting. She'd had a Styrofoam cup of coffee, and when the producers looked at each other and told her, as kindly as they could, that *a big record producer from the mainland sweeping a local girl off her feet* was a cliché, the cup trembled in Eleanor's hand. She spilled hot coffee on her thumb. And she'd said, with her voice all funny, Well, originally he wasn't a record producer. He wasn't? No, not originally. What was he, originally? No, it's too silly. Tell us. It's expensive. Tell us. It's impractical, dangerous, you couldn't get anyone to do it. But originally you had something different? Well, I see him falling from the sky. This beautiful man. He's handsome, strange-handsome not ordinary-handsome, and he's got a beautiful body. Beauty is good. We should celebrate beauty, and he's naked, that's the hard part, he's naked. Naked skydivers, they have them. There are such things. There was an ad in the *Telegram*, and my friend, Sadie, she decided she wanted to jump when she saw the ad. She wanted something big and dangerous. Just their bums in the paper with the parachutes wafting behind, a promotional ad. Sadie had to do a one-day course, how to land, bend your knees, and then there she was hanging on to the wing, the guy in the plane yelling at her, Jump, and her yelling back, Jump? And him yelling, Jump! And her still yelling, Jump? And finally the guy in the plane, he leaned out and he just edged her feet off the step with the side of his shoe, he basically pushed her feet off the step, and she let go, and that was it. So Sally — my character, Sally — is driving along a country road and she pulls over because she sees something, she gets out, and it's a naked skydiver. The whole thing is about fate. Big theme, fate. Sally feels fated to be with him. She watches him fall, her hand over her eyes to block the sun. And he lands, and rolls, and gathers up the parachute, and lopes over to her, he's loping. He's out of breath. Buck naked. A naked babe. There's this big field behind them and the sun, you know, going down.

The producers looked at each other, looked at Eleanor, We could do that. You could? We could do that, yes. You could do a naked skydiver? We could, yes, we could.

Gabrielle comes around the corner of the house, whacking the grass with a cracked broom handle. There was a scream for attention in each whack. She has lost one of the gold earrings her grandmother gave her. She wants to be absolved. She leans on Eleanor, rocking gently.

How's my girl, says Sadie.

What, Eleanor asks Gabrielle. What do you want? What? Gabrielle won't mention the missing earring. We have heard enough about the earring, thinks Eleanor. She was too young for gold. Eleanor is tired of Gabrielle. Tired of the wedding. Tired of losing things. She wants it to be tomorrow already. Her neck, the back of her neck, she realizes, is tired.

Hi, Sadie, Gabrielle says. Then she grabs Sadie around the waist in a fit of passion, burying her face.

I love you so much, Gabrielle says.

Are you having a good time at the wedding, honey, Sadie says.

Gabrielle rocks harder, stamps her foot.

Eleanor says, What?

Nothing.

Tell me.

Nothing. My earring, she whimpers.

You're impossible, Eleanor says. Philip comes out and sits beside them.

What's the matter with her?

The earring your mother gave her. Philip rubs his hand over the stubble on his chin.

The French, he says, are sometimes full of crap. Do you get that feeling?

Is it crap, Sadie says.

Philip says, But still, I'm like you, Sadie, I prefer the French.

Where's Maurice, Eleanor says.

He's showing Constance the dish he made for the wedding. Seaweed something or other.

We'll have to eat seaweed, Eleanor says, how gloomy.

Nobody has to eat anything they don't want to, Sadie says.

He's very clear about that. It's part of his *thing*, his whole thing. He thinks it's totally fucked up to eat out of politeness. And you don't ever lie, or make promises; that's also part of his thing.

We all have a *thing*, Eleanor says. If someone makes a dish you eat it, that's my thing.

Philip says, I'm not eating seaweed.

Or marry for convenience, says Sadie, you never do that, according to Maurice, even if you need citizenship to get a job so you can stay in the country and be with your lover whom you supposedly love.

I'm eating it, says Eleanor.

Or marry for any reason. Or have children, because that's a promise in itself. Never making a promise is part of Maurice's thing too. Although he loves children, says Sadie.

I also love children, says Eleanor, children are also part of my *thing*. Staying married is part of my thing. And just generally being nice to people. I believe in *being nice*.

Philip grabs Constance's dog, who is trotting by and stares into his eyes.

This dog wants to tell me something, Philip says.

Maurice loves other people's children though, says Sadie. He loves this little girl for instance. She gives Gabrielle an extra squeeze.

Philip says, I think the dog is starting to look like Nicolas Cage.

Eleanor says, Try new things, right? Isn't that right Philip? My god, there's a whole ocean of seaweed out there.

They shot the skydiving scene during a blizzard on the Bally-Halley golf course. The man they'd gotten to play the part was strikingly beautiful. Eleanor had said, You have a beautiful face. He was surprised to hear it. He'd been a weightlifter, said his thigh had once been twenty-eight inches around, he couldn't buy a pair of pants. His body was a separate thing, a thing by itself, he said while folding a Caesar salad into his mouth. He wasn't successful as an actor, had turned to repairing fridges, which is what his father did. A part comes up every now and then, he says. A part like this. She can tell he doesn't think much of nude skydiving. Of course, there's a stuntman to do the actual dive. But the actor must run across the field without his clothes.

Costume had sewn tiny heating pads into the straps of the parachute, but he was nude in the snowstorm. All the crew in knee-length eiderdown, the actor completely nude, running through the snow, gathering the parachute behind him. Eleanor hadn't written a storm but there it was. The shoot had been postponed and there was the storm. Two women waited outside the scope of the camera with thick blankets. The hulking actor trembling with frostbite. Everybody averting their eyes from his purple dick. The director called cut, and the girls ran up to the naked actor and flung the blankets over him and there was a consultation.

What the hell? I thought that was good, he called out over the field, hopping from foot to foot. Someone wiped his nose.

Snot? Snot on my goddamn face? I do the best goddamn performance of my *life* and there's *snot* on my face. Come on, let's do this thing, let's do this thing, he yelled.

The first time Philip cheated on her, if you can call it that, when it's out in the open, when there's an understanding: Eleanor and Philip had gone to a movie together, and afterwards they sat in the car, which was parked facing their house. It was raining, and the yellow clapboard of the three-storey house wiggled and snaked.

Philip said, There's something I forgot to tell you. When I was in Montreal for that conference, two years ago. I told you about the jazz, and the weather.

You told me about that, she says.

On the last night we were all going to a party in a hotel room. This woman and me, this very beautiful woman, we got into the elevator together. It was late at night. And we got out on the wrong floor. We were talking, about the conference, papers we'd heard. We got out in front of a floor-to-ceiling window, a whole wall of glass. And there was the city in front of us, spread as far as you could see, the lights. It was so beautiful. It shocked me. And I said, How beautiful. And this woman, she touched my hand, and she said, Yes, let's get a room.

He turned the car on and let the wipers clear the glass for two swipes, and their house was solid again, the clapboard straight, and the car filled with music, the radio was on loud, jazz, several horns, Miles Davis, maybe, and he turned it off. The house went soft, melting. She looked at him under the streetlight. A splatter of rainy shadows migrating over his nose, across his cheeks. His hand still on the key, looking straight ahead.

How does this confession change things? The yellow house is still yellow, the harbour beyond, the Atlantic Ocean, the rain hitting the street so hard it rises in a silver fur under the street-lights. It makes Philip a stranger, she thinks. Like in the beginning, when she sat on the frayed arm of the chair at Kibitzer's and just wanted to go home with him but was afraid. Maria Schneider making herself come without touching — they don't exchange names, she and Brando, they just fuck while his wife lies in a coffin.

And you forgot to tell me this.

I decided not to tell you. I decided not to tell you, and then I forgot to tell you.

But that night, when I spoke to you on the phone from Montreal, she says. She tried to think of the night. He had called every night, waking her. She loved being dredged out of sleep, trawled into the bedroom. Out drinking, he'd said. A bunch of Newfoundlanders at the conference and his paper had gone well, he'd called to tell her something about flowers and stars. They had been drinking outside, it was an outdoor pay phone he called her from. Flowers had fallen into his beer, or birdshit. It was birdshit. Nothing about stars. There had been laughter in the background and she'd fallen back to sleep, blissful.

With great effort she speaks to Glenn Marshall: Last summer Gabrielle wanted a ladybug, but they're like grace, you can't will them, either.

Glenn rises from his chair and his snifter of brandy smashes. She sees it fall, hot amber coming up to the mouth of the glass like a jellyfish.

You prepare for grace, he says. Thomas Aquinas said, Get ready. That's his advice, prepare.

Yes, she thinks, you wait. She glances at the window, but she can't see Philip, he has moved into the kitchen. She thinks of her mother and the white mink, how much was lost when her father died.

Eleanor says, It's about a girl who comes through grief via a sexual awakening.

The story editor says, What does that mean?

She says, When my father died, because essentially this script is about my father. Pleasure is a kind of betrayal, to feel pleasure, any kind of pleasure, after a death. Because pleasure is life affirming, and to go on living, enjoying life, when someone you love has died is to accept their death. And acceptance is a kind of betrayal, is my thinking here.

The screenplay is a messy jumble. Everything out of order. Full of dream sequences (self-indulgent, according to the story editor), the death, snowstorms, pregnancy, a prison where Sandra teaches art to a young woman who had attacked someone with a hammer (of course it's all true, the screenplay tells exactly what happened, her mother struggling to get the lawnmower into the trunk of her car so she could mow her husband's grave and finally throwing it at the car with a superhuman burst of strength brought on by grief).

The story editor takes up a coloured marker and approaches a flip chart. He draws a timeline.

He says, A half-hour screenplay is twenty-four pages. I want the grief fully realized by page four. I want to see the character attempt to overcome grief three times by page twenty. Three failed attempts, but each time she gets closer. I want the sexual awakening on page twenty. By page twenty-four she has come through.

And who is the father, the story editor asks.

Who is he?

I mean who is he, really, the story editor says.

She remembers her father bringing a Portuguese sailor home for supper when she was seven so they could hear a foreign language. She feels a burst of tears coming, her nose. But she won't cry in front of the story editor. In the elevator she noticed his black turtleneck, his raglan, his polished shoes. He has uncapped the marker. Death has made her father finite. She could list all the things he was. Everyone else, this man with the marker, Philip wanting to leave her, Sadie working on her film, everyone else is changing.

Like what was his favourite food, says the story editor, who did he read. What did he take in his coffee. You have to know these things about your character.

Who was it Eleanor's father used to read before bed?

Harold Robbins. Eleanor can see Harold Robbins in raised gold script. Her father would fall asleep each night with the book open on his chest, having read only a page or two.

After her father died, Eleanor's mother had a nervous breakdown, and then began to see Doug Ryan. Eleanor first read Harold Robbins while her father was still alive, just two pages. Two forbidden pages when she was thirteen.

They had been jumping off the Ryans' wharf, knees tucked up. The smack. Plunging down through a tunnel of bubbles and the murkiness near the bottom of the lake, the mossy struts of the dock, underground springs spurting up, making warm pockets, remembering the eels balled together in the darkness.

Eleanor had known about sex, the facts, for a long time, of course. She had been kissed. (She'd just let her horse, a fine-boned pacer, out of the barn and the mare had bucked and reared, front hoofs pawing the clouds, neck tossing, back legs step-stepping in the deep snow, and Eleanor caught the yellow nylon rope snaking past her jeans, the mare yanking her arms, her hands burned by the rope, digging in her heels, her mother had company, and they'd brought their son, three years older than Eleanor, sixteen, he was drinking a cup of tea he'd taken from the house, standing in snow up to his knees, she had loved the horse, had spent winter evenings in the mare's stall with just a flashlight, the smell of linseed oil she used to clean the tack, the brushes, she knew the animal's body, the shiny black knees, the way to pick up the hoofs and remove stones with a pick, a flame of pink inside the right nostril, the wet snuffle of giant lips against her palm when she held out half an apple, the smell of manure, the molasses in the grain, the water bucket with a skin of ice, the blue salt lick, smell of horse in her hair, under her nails, outside trees creaking together, the starry, dark blue sky. Walking back to her house through the trees, all the while her family going bankrupt, the television murmuring, her father hitting the adding machine, hitting the adding machine, the washer going, piles of money in front of him, a dish with a

193

sponge for counting, the adding machine, until morning, when she woke and found him leaning on the counter looking through the kitchen window at the sun coming up. He had cut up a grapefruit for her breakfast with a maraschino cherry in the middle. He was drinking his instant coffee.

Catching the horse's nylon halter, kelly green, bright against the blue sky, white clouds, after coaxing the mare into stillness, the white of her eye, Danny Martin came up to her and kissed her lips, he took his time, she could feel the mare's breath on her wrist, he was holding the cup and he tasted of milky tea out there in the snowbank on a spring day, the snow creeping back off the pavement, the asphalt shiny, the horse.

For weeks after, months, she imagined the kiss while falling asleep, and when her father sat her down on the plaid sofa and took her two hands in his, cradled them between his, explaining they would have to sell the horse, his heart nearly broken, she could hardly remember why she had ever wanted one.)

Harold Robbins described being overcome. Sexually overcome. Losing control. To think that such a thing could happen to adults. Those who made the world stable. Even after the bankruptcy, when there were less treats in the cupboard and no new clothes for a long time, everything had a certainty.

She understood why she hadn't been allowed to read the Harold Robbins. Her parents hadn't wanted her to know, and knowing, she could feel herself crossing over, becoming adult.

Terrified of the eels, which were definitely thickly knotted under the wharf, kicking hard to the dazzling surface of the lake; but as soon as she gets there, thirteen-year-old Eleanor instantly forgets the eels, climbs up the slimy ladder to jump again, ribs heaving to catch her breath.

Mr. Ryan used to deep fry battered cod tongues and serve them with tartar sauce.

The men always had one specialty and they were praised for it as if it were a miracle. Doug's cod tongues.

Somewhere she has heard the story, a famous editor had given Harold Robbins an advance after receiving the first half of a novel. When the final half came in, it was an entirely different story. The characters had different names, different crimes, different lovers, different settings. But Robbins wouldn't change a word. His editor found him on the Riviera. Robbins wouldn't leave his yacht. A champagne glass held high, women in bikinis. The editor claimed it would destroy Robbins's career, published the novel as it was, and nobody noticed. It sold as well as all the other Harold Robbins books. People read for the sex and wealth.

Glamour, thinks Eleanor, and she remembers Mr. Ryan's plastic toothpicks with the Playboy bunnies at the tip, in silhouette, jutting breasts and ponytails, the tiny cheeks of their bums perched on the picks, sticking out of the cod tongues. Mr. Ryan was being ironic with the toothpicks, making fun of himself, his inability to let loose. But the toothpicks were also a parody of the desire to let loose; he didn't believe in letting go.

Mrs. Ryan sent her to the house for ice. Eleanor had left the wharf, wandered up through the raspberry canes, eating some, pressing her tongue into the nubbly thimbles. Spiderwebs in the shade of the spruce trees wobbling with droplets of an early morning rain. Her sister, Fran, stood near the sprinkler for hours, the lines of water hitting her bright bathing suit in a burry asterisk of mist (the bathing suit was blue with bananas all over, the things that suddenly come back to you!), the steely threads moving over Fran's scrunched eyes, down her throat, chest, protuberant belly, and thighs. Hitting the sharp bones of her ankles and resting there like silver spurs.

There was too much sun. The Ryans' house was empty. She opened the freezer and took out the metal tray of ice. In the living room she lay the tray on the TV and picked up a Harold Robbins novel from the shelf. She checked the bay window in the living room, looked out over the lawn. She could hear the Ryan children at the wharf. The crashes of their bodies on the water, shrill laughter.

Mr. Ryan, just outside on the verandah, preparing the cod tongues. Their parents drank so much in the middle of the afternoon, thinks Eleanor. All day, in the sunshine with the fireweed swaying, the mild breeze lifting clouds of seed into the air, and the dark spruce with ribbons of lake hanging in the branches. They had been rich briefly, then the construction company had failed. The sprinkler reaching her sister's feet, and then, mysteriously, the water had dried up, someone, somewhere, had turned off the tap, and Eleanor's sister opened her eyes and blinked in disbelief.

It's such a shock when someone dies, all that energy, angst, desire, memory, love, the sheer *propulsion*, amounting to nothing. She just wants the screenplay to capture that: the shock.

The Harold Robbins novel: Eleanor on the cusp of puberty,

small breasts, ears pierced with two ice cubes freezing the lobes, and then the sewing needle, a drop of blood; in the mirror, her earlobes as dark as cherries, burning, the delicate jiggle of the dark red stones in the gold settings, her grandmother's, the hot sting of the sewing needle through numbed flesh.

But I'd never read a word of pornography, she thinks.

She opens to the second-last page. A man is holding a gun, he has caught up with a woman he is going to kill. Eleanor can tell he has chased her through the five hundred pages, she has betrayed him again and again, and he comes back for more, they are in a room alone, his arm out straight, his finger on the trigger. (Maybe she should shoot Philip, blow his head off with a rifle, ruin Constance's wedding.)

I will be independent, she thinks. She feels alert, squares her shoulders, a cold breeze from the lake, the potluck is ending, she is out on the lawn by herself, had she fallen asleep? She checks her chin for drool. She wonders if Philip has been waiting for a specific date when he can leave, like Mrs. Ryan. Has he planned to leave her all along?

Grace was not bestowed, she realizes. Nothing. Was it something Philip decided one night, resolved, resigned himself to? Surely Mr. Ryan, arranging the bowls of tartar sauce, the toothpicks, the serviettes, must have known something was going to happen.

Eleanor's mother singing out: Doug's cod tongues, what a treat!

How unthinkable that he would one day be with her mother for a short time, he would, in his confusion after

Mrs. Ryan left, turn to Eleanor's mother, who was herself so disoriented with grief, so lost, how unthinkable on that particular sunny afternoon when Eleanor read pornography for the first time. As if the characters of the afternoon had stepped into a different novel halfway through. Her mother in Mr. Ryan's arms. Her father buried on a hill overlooking the ocean. Mrs. Ryan seeing a lawyer in British Columbia.

The man grips the gun. The woman takes out her hairpins. Her shiny mahogany hair tumbles over her shoulders. She begins to unbutton her blouse. The man breaks into a sweat, he tries to look away, but he cannot. The woman reaches behind and unzips her skirt, it falls to her ankles, the man is trembling. He tells her not to move. She stands before him in a black lace bra and panties, garters, and fishnet stockings. The woman reaches back and unhooks her bra. Out on the verandah Mr. Ryan lowers a basket into the boiling fat and a roar rises.

The woman says, Shoot me if you can, Eleanor moves her head, feels her earrings jiggle. The woman leaning against the wall, her breasts, the gleaming satin of her bra, Danny Martin's kiss. The man slowly lowers his arm, he cannot hold the gun out any longer. The gun drops from his fingers to the floor. The woman steps out of her skirt, walks across the tiles in her high heels, and steps into his arms. The screen door slams. Eleanor drops the book, kicks it under the skirt of the couch (the screen door slams, it's Constance, checking the garden for Eleanor). Mr. Ryan is surprised to see her. For a moment he stands on the other side of the room, basket of cod tongues. The eels are undisturbed, writhing together between the crevices of rock at the bottom of the lake.

The editor snaps the top back on his felt-tip marker. He taps the flowchart with it.

We should see the father, he says. Who was he?

Eleanor and Philip take Gabrielle home in a taxi before the reception. Apple air freshener. She meets the eyes of the driver in the rearview mirror. It's the same driver. The one with the different wife altogether. She grabs her lapel.

Gabrielle, look! But the ladybug is gone.

Eleanor's mother, Julia, comes to pick up Gabrielle. She's babysitting so Philip and Eleanor can have a night together.

She says, Yes, you do, you need it.

Eleanor's sister has shaved her head.

Why would she do a thing like that, Julia asks. Who will hire her now, a bald woman? It's dark in the house after the lake, after the wedding dress blaring like a trumpet, the tinfoil trays of food floating through the party like a school of capelin. Eleanor closes her eyes and sees the lake spitting sparks, soft sparks. A wedding is a sham, she thinks. Constance letting the screen door slam behind her. Shading her eyes to check the children, the dress lifting like the lip of a snowdrift.

Eleanor says, Mom, was that weasel white? That weasel that ran through the rungs of the dining-room chairs.

What weasel? There was no weasel.

Eleanor thinks of Amelia on tiptoe, reaching for Philip's ear.

I want nothing to do with Philip, she thinks. My life should have gone another way. Climbing hills in Nepal. But if there were no Philip, there would be no Gabrielle. She fills with a gutful of love for her daughter. Gabrielle's braids in her hands. Braiding her hair while it's wet. One loose strand near the temple.

Why can't Gabrielle stay here with her? Why can't she and Gabrielle curl up in bed and sleep and forget the reception? Forget Philip. If he wants to get loaded and sleep with someone, just let him go. Dusk, almost night, and she and Gabrielle could order fish and chips. All the rooms in the three-storey house dark, except the kitchen, salt and vinegar. She imagines a rumbling under the ocean around Australia, the coral reef bursting apart, bits of brittle coral flying into the sun like batons.

She feels a catch — and leave Philip to be drunk with that blond woman, dancing, pouring beer over each other's heads, and finally kissing? Glenn Marshall is wrong. You don't wait for grace, or anything, you make it happen.

The last time she had take-out she saw the cook, in whites, lift baskets of fries from the roaring fat and stop to tip a sickly bottle of Pepto-Bismol down his throat. Straight from the bottle, and drop it back into the breast pocket of his apron.

You go on, Julia says. Gabrielle is fine with me. You need a party.

Then Philip comes from the kitchen with a mug of ice cream.

Lots of people shave their heads, he says.

He puts a mound of ice cream in his mouth, leaning against the wall, and pulls the spoon out of his mouth slowly. The

mound of ice cream like a fossil of the roof of his mouth,
a soft steam. He sees Eleanor looking at his mouth and he
raises an eyebrow. Immediately she wants to be with him, get
drunk with him, dance, she is grateful that her mom is taking
Gabrielle.

Julia says, Was that the groom I saw on Prescott Street
directing traffic with two soup ladles? They got a picture of it,
someone did. He'll be nice by midnight. Say goodbye to your
mother, Gabrielle. Kiss your mother goodbye.

Gabrielle throws her arms around Eleanor's neck, their foreheads gently knock, they look straight into each other's eyes.

Gabrielle whispers, I'm going to have chocolate.

Philip squeezes past them on the stairs. Eleanor sits and
listens to her mother's car doors. Hears the car pull away.

In the bathroom, Eleanor and Philip stand side by side brushing
their teeth. He pauses, his mouth foaming, the toothbrush still.

What were you and Glenn Marshall saying?

He gets in the shower. Eleanor undresses and gets in with
him. The water hits his shoulders hard. She lets her wrists rest
on his shoulder bones.

Then she kisses his chest, down his belly, until she is on
her knees. The water slides down his ribs like cloth. She makes
seams with her tongue. She puts her hand on his chest and the
water flows down her arm to the elbow, like an evening glove.
The hot water costing a fortune.

She says, Will I shave my legs?

Philip draws her up, takes her breast in his mouth.

The reception is at the Masonic Temple. There are perhaps two hundred people. More than the potluck — and the food. Constance has relatives from Heart's Desire, older women in shiny dresses, purples, scarlets, blues, clustered at long tables with pink streamers, and flowers and platters of marshmallow cookies, coconut-covered. Old-lady bifocals cutting the reflection of candle flames in half. They have brought trays and trays of food. Constance likes flowers. White roses at Christmas, always. Once on a winter afternoon she and Eleanor sat on the sofa and Constance said, I don't love him.

She picked a rose petal off the coffee table and smoothed it onto her chin. It hung there. It had been nothing more than a mood. It had passed. He asked her to marry him and she did.

But the relatives sit back as if they've done nothing. Arms crossed over broad chests, they sit back and the reflections of candle flames align in their glasses like the vertical pupils of cats, glowing from the dark corners of the Masonic Temple.

Sadie says to Eleanor, I kissed Constance on her satin shoulder. My lipstick on her wedding dress. My God, I'm not kidding. The whole dress is *ruined*.

There's a lineup at the bar. Eleanor sits and looks at the dance floor. Her eyes adjust to the dark. She can see Amelia Kerby's lamé flashing in the crowd. Her blonde hair is down now, curly. Her naked shoulder. She has someone by the tie. A chair screeches opposite her and Glenn Marshall gives her a beer.

She says, It's Glenn Marshall again.

He says, I don't dance.

Dance with me, Glenn, she says. She feels desperate.

That's exactly what I don't do, he says. It's Philip's tie. Here at a wedding with all of their friends. He is already drunk and she's holding him up by the tie. Constance drops into the seat beside Eleanor.

It can't last with Amelia, she says.

Things end, Eleanor says. She has heard this idea all her life — that things end — but took no interest. Now she tries it on to test its durability. She has always imagined she was building something with Philip. She had a do-good work ethic toward love. It was something you hammered, chainsawed, sized up with a spirit level, until it was absolutely durable and true. Along with something less substantial, a blithe, unexamined faith, airy as a cloud, that things were meant to be. There had never been a need to reconcile these conflicting notions.

She has no life experience, says Constance.

What do you mean, Eleanor says, she has her own apartment. She drives a rusting Volvo. What do you want? Eleanor's thinking of this girl hanging by her feet, bouncing like a Yo-Yo, up and down the side of a ravine on a bungee cord. Also her reportedly tidy apartment fitted with a Web-cam, and the grants that sustain her. Eleanor sees the lipstick mark on the gown's shoulder, a perfect full mouth.

Let's dance, Eleanor says.

What you need, says Constance, is a drink.

Eleanor tries to gather herself in, but she's too drunk. There's her face in the mirror, her cheeks, forehead. She's a skyful of

fireworks, a roller coaster, a birthday cake. She grips the bathroom sink but her shoulder hits a wall.

The sink is the wheel of a pleasure cruiser on a big sea and
she must turn it into the wave before they capsize. She's in the
basement of the Masonic Temple on Cathedral Street in downtown St. John's, Newfoundland. It's a steep hill, the harbour, the
cliffs, the North Atlantic, a sheer drop (the Grand Banks), and
nothingness. She clings to the sink. Everybody at the wedding,
two floors above — dancing, shouting, drinking beer — has
been washed out to sea in a wave shot through with tuna and
capelin and electric eels, especially Frank Harvey with his
flamboyant tie, and Dave Hogan who drives to Florida in a
Tilley hat, and Matthew Shea who puts his thumb over the
top of his beer spraying Gerry Pottle, who holds out his hands
going, What'd I do? What'd I do? And Matthew's wife with a
daiquiri held above one shoulder saying, Matthew, that's so
unim*press*ive. Amelia Kerby just now smacked Philip's shoulder
with the back of her hand and was ambushed by silent jerks
of laughter — all of them are depending on Eleanor to alter the
course of the evening, to drag the sink hard in the other direction, until she's lifted off her feet. She has to bring them into
port. She won't abandon her post, even in the face of this brick
shithouse of a wave. How had she gotten so drunk, she had
only been drinking.

If she could count how many beers in the afternoon, but it
was the gin. The gin was insubstantial and avid, intrinsically
cold, like reptile blood. At some point in the evening the word
juniper had seemed like a self-contained poem. There is no

turning back, they can only brace themselves. She has begun to think of herself as them. She's the entire wedding party, and the city beyond. Dragged out to sea.

The face in the mirror is starting to look exactly like her, she's coming into herself too fast. Philip was dancing with Amelia when Eleanor careened out of the banquet hall, down the musty staircase, platform heels, rickety handrail.

The bathroom floor buckles in the grip of a swell and Eleanor is flung against the wall and hauls herself, hand over hand, up the roiling radiator to the cubicle. She lets her head drop against the door of the stall. If she can just hang on she will reach her purest self. She may have to puke to get there. Something pure, like a breeze through the pines of the Himalayas. She'd camped once in a forest in Kashmir. Slippery pine needles slicked the paths. At night the guide called from his tent: Watch out for the snow leopards!

The outer door bangs and she feels it reverberate in her bum. Two women have burst into the bathroom.

Sadie says, Someone in there?

I am, says Eleanor.

And who is I am? A fairy in a CBC Christmas special once when she was fourteen. They chromokeyed her so she floated over a frozen lake, pointed toes wiggling, to touch down beside an ice-fishing folksinger who grabbed up his guitar to play a carol. She'd once knit a long red scarf. Rode in a mock fox-hunt. They had several bloodhounds, but it was Eleanor's French poodle, Monique, who treed the old fur hat doused with musk hidden in the crotch of a birch. She'd hitchhiked the island maybe seven times. She'd taken all kinds of lessons: raku, clay animation, Spanish, watercolour painting. The secret to a successful watercolour is to use many, many transparent veils of colour. This is also the secret to raku, vegetarian cooking, synchronized swimming, and being very, very drunk when your husband is dancing with a bubblehead from British Columbia, or from anywhere for that matter. It is not the secret to flying trapeze, belly dancing, waitressing at the Blue Door, or being very, very drunk when your husband picks up the fine gold necklace that lies flat against Amelia's collarbone with his lips. There is no secret for that. You must carom like the silver balls in a pinball machine, spitting sparks with each wall your forehead smacks. You must grip the wheel with both hands, you must pick a star and aim true.

Eleanor realizes that she's unable to puke. She is bloated with woe. There's so much woe. Puking she can forget. She drank; she is drunk. These honest statements grip hands like used car salesmen. She straightens up and steps out of the cubicle.

Sadie is holding her wrist to Constance's nose.

It's called Celestial Sex, says Sadie, everybody's wearing it. Both women turn to face Eleanor and then lurch forward to catch her.

Eleanor says, Constance, your dress. It's smeared with lipstick.

The women grip Eleanor's shoulders just as the tiled floor slants toward her chin. They squash her between them.

Eleanor lets her face fall into Sadie's cleavage. Eleanor wants to let go the wheel. Let them dash against the cliffs, let the ocean crunch them in its rotten chops. She closes her eyes, nuzzling Sadie's breasts with her nose, and plummets. She's a jellyfish pulsing through infinite inkiness, the ordinary encumbrances giving way: bone, jealousy, the smell of smoke and shampoo, the stinky emerald cloud of pot that still hangs over the cubicles, the way her mother stood a boiled egg in her wedding ring, her father smoothing cement with a trowel, Eleanor's horse pawing the clouds with his front hoofs, the pink of his nostril, the white of his eye, good olives, her name, streets, books, aspirations, socks, coins, hair clips, all of it giving way. Then she grabs Sadie's spaghetti strap and drags herself back up, surfacing amid the bagpipe screams of the toilets. What it means to be human is spelling itself in the grey mould spreading over the ceiling. She must speak. She will hint at the immanent peril. Sadie can take it.

Philip is all over her, Eleanor says.

Downer, says Constance.

Remember who you are, says Sadie.

She had imagined herself in love lots of times. Sometimes she knew she wasn't and fought to convince herself, saying, See? That must be love, see? He's done this, you felt that way, you thought of him while making mashed potatoes, you thought of him when the chain came off your bike, you thought of him.

Knowing she wasn't in love but not knowing what love was and thinking, it might be this. It might be she and Sam Crowley hidden under the dripping laburnum, the poisonous flowers bright at dusk, his kid sister standing on the pedals of her bike, whizzing by like a thought through the liver-coloured maple trees. Clem Barker tearing the condom wrapper with his teeth. Paul Comerford, between the rolls of unlaid carpet, leaving the impression of his bum in a pile of sawdust. Eli Pack kissed the back of her neck, and led her to his back seat, his finger and thumb circling her wrist loosely, but it might as well have been a handcuff, because she couldn't have said no if she tried. Then on a plaid blanket covered with cat hair. Eleanor is all of this. Tom O'Neill in a field of wild roses he claimed was inhabited by fairies. Stoned with Harry McLaughlin so his fingers stirred up a trail on the inside of her thigh like an oar in a phosphorescent shoal. When she was sixteen, Rick O'Keefe held her against his greasy coveralls, a fresh whiff of gasoline. With Brian Bishop in a motel in Port Aux Basques, a snowstorm, they'd missed the ferry. Afterward they devoured a bucket of Kentucky Fried Chicken. Wiped their greasy mouths in the tail of the bedsheets. Mark Fraser, on a bale of hay, a surprise because he'd sworn all summer he hated her. Hunched over, he had flicked a Bic lighter until it ran out of juice and he'd tossed it and gathered her roughly, the hay pricking through her jeans, he'd knocked her riding hat so the elastic tugged at her throat and then he had stopped, astonished. He'd whispered, You're a nice girl, as if he'd opened her like a parcel. Donny White had let a line of sand spill from his fist into her belly button, up her stomach, and over the triangles of her glossy orange bikini. Mike Reardon had rubbed his jeans against her bum, pressing her hipbones against the counter until she rinsed the last cup.

Sadie tugs Eleanor's dress roughly, this way and that, as if she were making a hospital bed. Constance trawls the bottom of her tiny purse until she draws out a lipstick, lethal as a bullet. She dismantles it and screws up the explosion of colour. She grips Eleanor's jaw and covers the pouting bottom lip and says, Rub them together. Sadie has got her by the hair, dragging a punishing brush through so fast that Eleanor's scalp yelps.

Listen, Sadie says, it's only that *yahoo* Amelia Kerby, *who cares?*

And then it rises in her, the wave, plowing up through the guts of the evening, up through her platform shoes, grinding her kneecaps to dust, into her thighs, a spraying granite of surf hitting her crotch, stomach, her breastbone splintering, all blown apart.

I care, wails Eleanor, I lo-huv-huv-huv-huve him.

She and Philip bought a house around the bay. The grass up to their waists. Tiger lilies. Fireweed. Crabapples. Philip pulled over on the side of the road and rolled down the window.

Why are we?

Shhh.

Can we just.

Shhh.

He'd pulled over next to a copse of whispering aspen. The car filled with the leafy, percipient surf. The wind blew, and the leaves showed their silver undersides as if the tree had been caught naked and was trying to cover up.

And the wave withdraws. Eleanor is still standing. The bathroom is lustral, the fluorescent lights thrumming like an orchestra of didgeridoos. Sadie and Constance are angels with tangy auras like orange zest. They are springtime, a Scandinavian polar bear swim, they are the girls in the cake, Isadora Duncan, they've bested the mechanical bull, they're electricity after an outage, they are her friends. Eleanor is okay. She's okay. She's going to be *fine*.

I will fight, Eleanor says.

There you go, says Sadie.

She had awakened in Philip's apartment, ten years ago. Trembling, partly from the hangover, but mostly from fright. She knew she was in love. How terrible. She could still feel his finger tracing the elastic of her underwear. She lay on her back, her arms over her head, her wraparound dress — he had untied the string at her hip and lifted the fabric away, and untied the other string inside the dress, beneath her breast. Little bows he pulled slowly. So she lay there in the black bra and underwear. His finger moved from one hip to the other, tracing the elastic. It was that finger moving over her belly that tipped her. It spilled her over. A car roared up the steep hill outside the apartment and squealed its tires, and the squeal felt like her heart, as if her heart were tearing around the corner of an empty street in the last sleeping city on the Atlantic. A brass candle holder crusted with wax. A Fisher Price telephone with a glowing orange receiver. She had stumbled over it on their way in and the bell rang clear. When she awoke in the morning she came into herself. Sunlight piercing the weave of a rosy curtain, the wardrobe door hanging open, his jeans on the back of a chair, the red suspenders sagging, exhausted from the effort of holding him back.

Eleanor jerks the wine glass back and forth as if it is a gear shift manoeuvring her across the room. She stumbles forward and grabs Sadie's arm.

She says, This is the sort of drunkenness it takes a lifetime to achieve. I must actualize my potential before it wanes. I may never achieve this clarity of purpose again as long as I live.

Sadie says, You might regret this.

Whose side are you on?

I'm just saying, in the morning.

Because I'm ready here.

In the clear light of day.

If I'm all alone, just say so.

You're not alone, it's just I'm thinking a glass of water, a Tylenol, forty winks.

So you're with me?

Whatever you say.

You're in?

I'm in.

Let's actualize.

Eleanor drags Sadie across the dance floor, grabbing at dresses and suit jackets to stay standing. Finally she taps Amelia on the shoulder. Amelia turns.

You, she says. Amelia smiles.

Eleanor says, You, you, you. Where is your husband?

I have no husband.

That's right, says Eleanor. She grins triumphantly.

Your boyfriend, then, where's he?

It was nothing, Amelia says, my last boyfriend.

Nothing? It was nothing? Okay, the one before that.

Him too, nothing. She makes a sound, Pfft.

Okay, the one that broke your heart, where is he?

Pfft, says Amelia.

Pfft? Pfft? says Eleanor. She suddenly rests her forehead on Sadie's shoulder. It's true the girl has no life experience. There is no way to make an impression on her. There is no way to dent that lamé. She is what she appears, bubbly and handsome with a certain talent for academic lingo and a healthy bank account. Eleanor feels no match.

Well, you've started it now, Sadie says.

Eleanor rouses herself. She will do it then, if she's forced, finish this girl off, although already a new clarity has befallen her. The girl has nothing to do with it. Where, she wonders sadly, is Philip. Who is he? How can she remind him who he is?

I mean the boyfriend, then, says Eleanor, who took his bare hands and tore your flesh and pried the bones of your ribs apart and reached up and tore your beating heart out with his fingernails and then put it in his mouth and chewed it up and swallowed it. And then smiled at you with your own blood dripping down his teeth.

Here Eleanor mimes as she speaks (a trick she's learned from Frank Harvey) a pulsing heart in her fist. She mimes the heart almost slipping out one end of the fist, but catching it, cupping it in both hands. The heart truly appears to be pulsing in her cupped hands. She looks at Sadie, astonished by her own facility. Sadie looks astonished too. Eleanor is holding Amelia Kerby's slithering, tough little bungee-jumping heart. And then, snarling like a dog, Eleanor chews the tough meat of Amelia's heart. She wipes her mouth with the back of her hand.

That boyfriend, she says.

Um, that's never happened to me, Amelia says. Sadie puts her arm around Amelia and gives her a squeeze.

I think what my friend is trying to say is stay away from her husband. He's a little confused right now, but they have a kid and a really great marriage and you don't want to inadvertently fuck that up, now, do you?

At four-thirty in the morning everyone forms a circle around the bride and groom on the beer-soaked dance floor. They hold hands and sway violently, some of them fall over and the other side of the circle drags them up from their knees. Then that side, because of the exertion, topples and they must be hauled back on their feet. They rush into the centre of the dance floor, joined hands raised over their heads. The circle rushes in and pulls out. The bright dresses like bits of glass and sparkle in a kaleidoscope that fall to the centre with each twist of the lens and drop away. Blue stage lights splash over them, up the walls, across the ceiling, the floor. The bride and groom hug the guests, making their way around the circle.

Constance holds Eleanor's head in her hands tightly, she presses her cheek against Eleanor's cheek, and her face is wet and hot. She draws back and the red light falls over her, splinters of purple searing from the sequins in her veil, on the bodice of her dress.

I love you, Eleanor, she says, I love you. And I love your husband too. And I love my husband. I love everybody's husband.

She lets go of Eleanor's face and falls into the arms of the man next to Eleanor. Ted grabs Eleanor and holds her. He has a beer in each hand and the bottles chink behind her back.

Eleanor tugs Philip's shirtsleeve.

Come home with me?

Not yet, he yells.

She is lying in bed waiting for him. It's 7:32 a.m. She lies still. There is a fear rushing around in her body. She remembers her mother calling a few years ago about the weasel. Eleanor can feel that mink fear rippling through her body because she fell in love the first night she slept with Philip and after that she fixed on him.

A body slams against a wall and falls onto the opposite wall of the porch. It's either Philip or the three Norwegian sailors who rent the attached house. The angry saints with their haloes of white hair and steady brawling.

Philip lurches to the banister, wraps his arms around it as if it were the mast of a capsizing ship.

He looks up at her.

He says, I went to Signal Hill in a Cadillac.

Eleanor is standing at the top of the stairs.

We stopped at the Fountain Spray to buy candy necklaces and we had a giant bottle of wine. I bit the necklaces off all the women's necks. He burps.

Glenn Marshall's neck too. Spectacular Sam was there. That guy who dances on broken glass. Do you remember that guy? He does a lounge lizard thing, and the Caribbean drums.

He lunges past her and she follows him to the bedroom.

He says, Spectacular Sam poured cognac over broken beer bottles on the parking lot of Signal Hill. Lots of smashed glass. He lit it, fell into a trance, and danced on it with his bare feet. Then he knelt and scooped the glass up in his hands and splashed his face with it, and drops of blood came up all over his face. You know, there was the sun too, coming up.

Philip struggles for a long moment with the buttons of his shirt, tipping slowly on his heels like a punching clown in a breeze. He sighs and rips the shirt open. Buttons hit the wall above the lamp. He falls onto the bed.

She gets up to turn off the light, but he grabs her arm.

Stay here, he says. Stay here.

Acknowledgements

This book is for Steve.

I am grateful to the following people who read these stories with love in one fist and a hatchet in the other. Thank you all for the sound and cacophonous advice: Ramona Dearing, Steve Crocker, Susan Crocker, Michael Crummey, Jack Eastwood, Mark Ferguson, Michael Jones, Mary Lewis, Nan Love, Beth Ryan, Medina Stacey, Larry Mathews, Lynn Moore, Claire Wilkshire, Michael Winter.

For being as exacting and generous an editor as one could possibly hope for, I am grateful to Martha Sharpe.

Thank you to my big, gorgeous, rowdy, loving family.

Versions of these stories first appeared in the literary journals *Best Canadian Fiction, The Malahat Review, The Fiddlehead, The Journey Prize Anthology, This Magazine, TickleAce,* and the anthologies *Hearts Larry Broke* (Killick) and *Turn of the Story* (Anansi). Thanks to the editors of these publications.

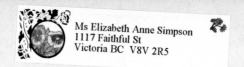

OPEN

Ms Elizabeth Anne Simpson
1117 Faithful St
Victoria BC V8V 2R5

Thank you to the Canada Council and The Newfoundland and Labrador Arts Council whose support made this book possible.

62° 2:20 PM
Friday April 18